ANAMNESIS

ANAMNESIS

A NOVEL

NOEL ZAMOT

Atabey Press
New Port Richey, Florida

First Edition.

ISBN: 979-8-9877112-7-9 (ebook)
ISBN: 979-8-9877112-8-6 (Paperback)

For those who seek

"Anyone not shocked by quantum mechanics has not yet understood it."

— NIELS BOHR, NOBEL LAUREATE IN PHYSICS (1922)

"Consciousness cannot be accounted for in physical terms. For consciousness is absolutely fundamental."

— ERWIN SCHRÖDINGER, NOBEL LAUREATE IN PHYSICS (1933)

"It [is] not possible to formulate the laws of quantum mechanics [...] without reference to the consciousness."

— EUGENE WIGNER, NOBEL LAUREATE IN PHYSICS (1963)

ANAMNESIS

anamnesis | ˌanəmˈnēsəs |
noun
1 the remembrance of a past life or previous existence.
2 *In Christian tradition* the sacred act of recalling the Passion, Resurrection, and Ascension of Christ.

From the Greek ***anamnēsis*** 'remembrance'.

INTRODUCTION

In the early twentieth century, discoveries in science cracked open reality. Einstein bent space and time; while Bohr and Schrödinger uncovered a quantum world where probability ruled over certainty. This was a golden generation, with each new breakthrough rewriting the rules of nature, their Nobel Prizes the milestones of a revolution.

One experience, however, perplexed everyone. In the famous "double-slit experiment," scientists fired electrons at a thin metal screen with two parallel apertures. By all expectations, the result should have been straightforward. Instead, it revealed something impossible: *results changed in the presence of an observer.*

The implication was staggering: *awareness shaped reality.*

Since then, we've developed complex equations to describe the effect — but not explain it. We are no closer to understanding why or how consciousness can alter the fundamental realities of our universe.

A century later, the puzzle remains unsolved.

CHAPTER I

There's a moment in every man's life when he looks in the mirror and hates who stares back.

That moment had come and gone for Prospero Jones. Tonight, after a lifetime of failure, he'd do something about it.

He snapped the hair clippers to life with a dull buzz, hacking a path through his thinning hair. Bald was not his best look, but faded gray would not cut it for his last hours on earth. If he was going to end a life of failure and shame, he might as well look the part.

He let off the pressure over bumps, then finished the job with a disposable razor. The mess on the floor would soon be sucked up by the vacuum. Only his hair, mixed with the dirt from his house, would outlive him. He wondered if the next tenant of his crappy apartment would ever know.

He toweled off and rubbed his head in approval. The cops wouldn't find a scraggly old man—if they found anything at all. He'd look good on his way out.

He tidied up the floor and sink before slipping on a t-shirt and coat, then reread the card he'd left on the breakfast table.

His final note was simple and to the point—like his life should've been.

I'm sorry I failed everyone. Please move on. Don't grieve for me. I am happier now.

That last one was a lie, but read better than "There is nothing left, and nothing beyond."

The walk to the bridge passed in a buzz. Not from the pills —those would hit in a few minutes—but from the sudden vibrancy of life, something that in minutes would no longer matter. Death, he'd decided, would not be a crucible of pain, but a shutting of the light. It struck him as strange that his consciousness—the single aspect of his world in which he could place complete faith—could be so quickly extinguished. Loss of awareness, like the stupor of anesthesia or dreams, would snuff out whatever had once been him. And whatever had once been him, had not been enough.

That failure would end tonight.

Everything would soon be over. No more defeat, no more debt, no more loss. The date had been picked so as not to remind his ex-wife of Tabitha. Fifteen years had passed in an instant, and changed his life. Thirty days seemed enough time between anniversaries to dampen Jeanine's pain. A decade hence, she would forget him but continue to grieve their still-born daughter. From a cosmic standpoint, it seemed back-ward. As a parent, he understood.

Not a single vehicle stopped to ask why a lone figure walked to the boat launch by the swamp bridge late on a moonless Tuesday. To others, he was just one of the many drunk homeless looking for shelter along the riverbanks off the Florida Gulf Coast. The cops would check in tomorrow, looking for derelicts and drunks. Part of him hoped the gators wouldn't have their way, and he'd be found, shriveled and cold, as authorities dredged the bottom of the Anclote for the missing. But the best outcome, he knew, would be for him to end up as gator shit days from now. The ring, the note, the little trinkets he'd saved for the adoption—those would be enough to tell his story. Not that anyone would care about it in another year, or another hour.

The crunch of gravel woke up a sleeping figure yards from the shore. He knew these people well, neighbors from casing the site so many times in the past month.

"No worries, Rex. It's just me. I'm going for a dip."

"Y'alright, son?" Rex sounded groggy and drunk. He'd be fine.

"Super good," Prospero lied, and felt a lump in his throat. "Cold wakes me up."

"See ya in the mornin'." Rex rustled into his tarp, next to the shopping cart holding his only possessions.

Thus ended his last conversation with another human: another escapee from a failed life, another man dying in the fall from relevance to obscurity.

He glanced behind him one last time as he neared the riverbank. A karaoke bar, closed on Tuesday nights, loomed in the darkness. One figure paused on the bridge for an instant before moving on, oblivious of what would happen next. The last witness to his end had walked away, leaving him utterly and completely alone.

He took a deep breath and stepped into the murk.

Cold shot up his leg. He scanned the water for the beady glow of gator eyes: the small ones were smart enough not to go for chaos on shore, and the big ones would wait. A shiver— was it cold, or fear?—woke him enough to delay the dulling of the pills. He needed to swim far out, go to sleep, and drown.

His coat, engorged with water, weighed him down. For a

moment, he panicked. He had no interest in drowning while awake. All the bullshit on the suicide feeds about it being the best way to die was insane. He could not imagine being conscious as his lungs filled and he struggled for air, smothered by water. So he breathed in deep, pushed down the panic, and swam.

His entire life came down to these last moments, a few minutes of awareness, emotion, and regret. Every sensation seemed magnified, as if Death gave him one last chance to decide. Had he taken care of everything? The insurance, the letter, the meager offerings to the one person who made him smile? These and other questions would never be answered. They'd fade when the chemicals took his attention and his will. The shutting off of the light would not be a switch, but a dimming of his soul.

He treaded water for seconds or minutes until the desire to paddle back to life passed, and the brackish water enveloped him like a dead womb. The shivering crept up, unwelcome but expected, so he turned onto his back to float. He gazed up at the sky, unsullied by streetlights, or hate, or lies. The euphoria of the endless universe spread into him like dawn.

Life was beautiful. It just hadn't been for him.

Something tugged at his feet—an animal with no concept of its pecking order, a mindless thing that would end his life without thought or mercy. Terror fought against exhaustion, and he felt the first tendrils of his life vanishing, the cruelty and indifference of death, the precious futility at the end of life.

That's when a light enveloped him, a hand reached down, and everything went dark.

CHAPTER 2

"You awake?"

He opened his eyes, heart in his throat, and sat up.

He was alive. Or was this the afterlife? He squeezed his eyes to shunt away fatigue, but confusion remained, leaking into his mind like the light filtering into his bedroom. The bed —his bed—lay rumpled and cool, exactly as he'd left it. His clothes, wet with the filth of the bayou, seeped water into a corner.

A woman he'd never met sat in his only chair, facing him. He peeked under his covers and realized he was naked.

The woman stood up, feline and smooth. She wore no glasses or visors, so her eyes—hard, older, without mirth— cut through him. Maybe she was the devil, or an attendant at Purgatory. He did not imagine angels wore cropped hair instead of halos or wings.

"Who are you?"

"Here. Drink." She handed him a bottle of water, still unopened. Prospero had no reason to trust her, and her gaze suggested she agreed. Her hands, lean and strong, belonged to a woman who wasted neither time nor money on pampering. She seemed incapable of a smile.

Prospero snapped the cap open and drank the cool water in one gulp. If this were a simulacrum of the afterlife, he would've expected something better than convenience store water.

"What is going on?"

The woman raised an eyebrow. "You tried to kill yourself."

"I think the word is suicide. Did... I die?" The question sounded stupid as soon as he uttered it. "Where am I? Is this hell?"

The woman shook her head, smiling this time. "No. You're not dead. And you are not in hell. You're in your apartment." She wiped a finger across his windowsill. "And you have a lot of dust. It's really bad for allergies, you know that?"

"You haven't told me why you're here. What happened?"

"You tried to kill yourself. I pulled you out."

"Are you a cop?"

She chuckled and shook her head.

"How did you find me?"

She waved the question away. "That bayou water stinks, by the way. And you don't have laundry in your apartment."

"I know that," he spat. "Who are you? Why did you pull me out?"

"My name is Andromeda Vestal. People call me Andy."

"What kind of a name is Andromeda?"

Andy sneered back. "What kind of a name is Prospero?"

He shook his head. "Parents liked Marlowe, I guess. You still haven't told me what happened. *Andy.*" He gathered the sheets around him in shame. Andy Vestal was in her late forties, lean and strong, lacking the expected grace or softness of a woman her age. Years ago, someone might've fallen for her; a quick fantasy for a desperate teenager or wistful retiree. Whoever she was, it appeared she hadn't pissed her life away: she was fit and strong, wore no jewelry or digital augmentation, and did not appear to even own a phone.

"Why thank you," she said, as if reading his thoughts. "Here." She tossed a wad of clothing at him and walked out.

Prospero dressed — t-shirt, undies, hiking pants — and checked his reflection in the mirror. He'd forgotten he'd shaved his head.

The sun's rays struggled to pass through windows dirty with neglect. Andy sat at his breakfast table, reading the note. His ears burst in shame.

"That's none of your business." He snatched the card away.

Andy stared as if considering a dense child. "Actually, it is very much my business."

"Look, I appreciate you pulling me out of the bayou, but I'm a little freaked out by all this." He gestured around his apartment, unsure of what he meant. Someone had rescued and returned him to his crappy apartment, lost in a forgotten town of a state he hated. Whatever choices he'd made to land here had led to failure. Months ago, he'd decided to end the shame. Now, he couldn't even kill himself.

"You'll see why," she said with a nod, which made no sense.

"You still haven't told me why you're here. Why did you pull me out of the water?"

"Because you were drowning."

"And you interrupted me! I wanted to end it. I wanted to end everything." He held up the card. "For reasons that are none of your business!"

"You are very much my business, Prospero Jones." She

stood up, lithe and smooth, like a seasoned predator. "You were going to die. And we can't allow that."

"Who the hell is we? Church?" He stepped back, mouth agape. "Oh shit! Jeanine sent you, didn't she? Didn't want the insurance. Just the alimony." He crumpled the card, flushing with shame and anger. "You can tell her that no one will hire me now that—"

"I'm not here for your alimony, Prospero Jones, or your insurance. I rescued you from drowning because you have to save the world."

CHAPTER 3

He stared for a moment, then burst into laughter.

"Save the *what*?"

"The world, Prospero." Andy gestured around her. "That includes this apartment, which you should do a better job of keeping clean."

He held her gaze, and when she didn't burst into laughter herself, pointed at the door. "Okay, thanks for your time. I'd like you to leave."

Andy shrugged and stood. "This is probably all a bit much. We'll be in touch."

"Yeah, it is a bit much, and no, we won't." He grabbed a hoodie from the mess on the futon and opened the door. "I don't know who you are and why you pulled me out. But the last thing I need is a con when my life is falling apart. So please." He gestured outside.

Andy paused, then stepped toward the kitchen sink. "You shouldn't leave dirty dishes behind when you plan on killing yourself. It's a nice touch to leave everything clean."

"Forgive me for not tidying up after my last meal. Please. Door's that way. You need to go."

She traced a finger over the dishes in the sink, and a tang of ammonia wafted behind her. Maybe she really *was* a demon.

"We'll be in touch," she said as she stepped through the door.

"No, we won't. I don't need this in my life. No offense." He stuffed his hand in his hoodie. The floor tile, chilly despite the warm night, stung his bare feet.

"See you soon, Pete." She turned and walked down the stairs.

Fury shot through him. "How'd you know that? You talked to Jeanine, didn't you?"

"No, Prospero," she said, not turning back to face him. "I just know."

He slammed the door before she walked out of sight, then peeked out the window to follow her. Andy, if that really was her name, walked through the parking lot without looking back, then disappeared down the street.

He turned back, waving a hand to disperse the fading ammonia smell. He sneaked a glance as he reached out for the fridge and stopped.

The dishes were clean. Immaculately clean, as if someone had sent them through an autoclave instead of a dishwasher. He picked one up, expecting it to be radioactive or something.

They were warm. And spotless.

"What the...?"

This was a dream, or a nightmare. He shook his head, trying to wake up, and pounded his fists on the counter and sofa and chairs to test their existence. He wondered why his nightmares might focus on a taciturn middle-aged woman who avoided technology and cleaned dishes. Outside, palm trees and oaks rustled in a gentle dawn breeze. Leaden clouds mottled the sky, and beams of reflected city lights traced dusty shards in the still air.

Shame overcame him. Hours before, he'd tried to kill himself. He was so pathetic he'd even failed at ending his life. Prospero Jones dropped onto his second-hand futon sofa, one of the few things he owned in this crappy life, and cried.

Minutes later, after exhaustion replaced shame, he wiped his eyes dry and shuffled to his bedroom. He threw the stinking pile of wet clothes in the shower stall and opened the tap.

The hot water revived him. He lathered up twice, stomping on his clothes and hoping the suds would get rid of the bayou stench. Only hours after trying to kill himself, he had already lost weight, the only positive result from another very poor decision.

He wrung his clothes as best he could and dumped them into the sink before toweling himself dry. It was too humid to hang them outside. His coat would never dry on its own, but going to the laundry room was unbearable. The dark cave was one more reminder of his defeat, of how much he'd fallen. He stared at the clothes, willing the water to evaporate, to carry with it the memory of his stupidity from the previous night, and avoid another depressing trip to the laundry. He heard a roar, a far-off ringing in his ears, and shook his head. Now I'm losing my hearing, he thought.

It took him a few seconds to notice the steam.

He stepped back, almost slipping on the wet tile. He waved away the cloud emanating from the sink, turned on the fan, and opened the door. Steam billowed from the sink as if something were burning.

He ran to the kitchen, holding a towel around his waist, returning with the fire extinguisher. Amazing how one could remember things forgotten when situations dictated action.

He was about to pull the pin and blast the clothes when he noticed the rush of steam had stopped. Still holding the fire extinguisher, he reached out and touched the pile.

Bone dry. Not burnt, merely warm. Frost clung to the outside of the sink and to the bathroom walls.

He picked out the jacket, fluffed it up, and stuck his hand in a sleeve. The fabric had dried, the stench of the bayou replaced by a vaguely salty smell. His pants, socks, underwear, tech tee—everything he'd worn the night he planned to kill himself—felt dry, defying the freezing sink, denying any memory of last night.

The world swayed. He sat on the toilet seat, face in his hands, afraid he was going insane. He swallowed hard and squeezed his hands open and shut. Was the sound he heard a sign of a stroke? He stood up, balancing on each foot and grimacing in the mirror, as he might imagine someone checking for neurological damage. Satisfied he wasn't losing his mind, he put on clothes, grabbed his notebook, then walked out.

The sun peered through the clouds creeping in from the sea. He considered riding his bike to the coffee shop, but wasn't yet sure how physics worked in this new dreamworld. He wanted to know, with absolute certainty, whether he was alive or dead.

Only one person held the power to convince him—the one person he'd thought of the instant before dying. She was the only person who could still make him smile. These days, Prospero Jones had no one left—except for someone who barely knew him. That one person was the sole anchor in his life, whether or not she knew. She'd provide answers and evidence, the only being who could prove reality or snap him out of the dream.

He walked to Sirius Java, his hometown coffee shop, savoring the pang of evanescent thrill every time he opened the door. She caught his gaze after thanking a customer, and her smile blasted away every shred of loss.

"Hi Prospero!" Evangeline See stared for an instant, then burst into a giggle. "What did you do to your hair?"

CHAPTER 4

He stepped to the register and ran a hand over his head. "Morning, Evangeline."

"What did you do?" She stared at him with a wonder-filled smile. "To your head!"

"I, uh, needed a change."

She pursed her lips and tucked a lock of honey-blonde hair behind her ear. "Helluva change. Usual?"

"Yes, please."

"Haven't seen you in a few days. How's the book?"

Eighteen months after meeting her, Prospero still found it difficult to look Evangeline See in the eye. She was different from everyone else in the world, capturing him from the first moment. Evangeline—birder, barista, and poet—radiated joy into a desperate world. He could not remember a single time when she hid her attention behind glasses or visors or handsets, when she didn't smile, when her sky-blue eyes didn't light up with brilliance and possibility. She was strong and compact, blessed with no need for makeup or diet. She'd played softball in high school, soccer in college, and now toyed with a PhD in something that changed every month. Prospero thought she was the most beautiful being in all of creation.

He also suspected she might be young enough to be his daughter, a never-ending source of guilt and shame. He'd read enough to know this innocent infatuation would never end well. His admiration would forever remain platonic. He was destined to be nothing in Evangeline's life, although she would be everything in what remained of his.

"Going slow. I took a break from writing for a few days."

"You'll get back to it."

He allowed a sheepish smile. "Maybe I'll write it out longhand."

"The best writers do that." She winked, and his insides lurched. "I'll bring your drink out."

He sat at a small table under a window and clutched his black notebook. A week ago, in this very spot, he'd decided to end his life. Evangeline had taken a rare day off, which transformed the coffee shop from bright and welcoming into the crypt that fermented his dying thoughts. People drowning in worlds of their choosing surrounded him, every one unaware of his decision. Peeking into the insanity he'd written that day seemed absurd. He opened the book, unable to find the last page that held his dying wish, when he felt her.

"Here's your coffee," Evangeline sang.

"Thank you. Desperately need it today." He could sense her presence — her warmth, her scent, the sheer power of her eyes—even from afar. Was he going insane?

"Is everything okay?"

He nodded, shook his head, and nodded again. "I feel out of sorts. Like this... isn't real, you know?"

"I know. Sometimes it feels like life is just a chain of

disparate moments jumbled together. Like an endless Monday." She stood back, considering him with a toothy smile. "It's growing on me."

"What?"

"Your new look. I think bald men can still be handsome."

"Of course you would, dear," a bitter voice cut into him. "Daddy issues, anyone?"

Evangeline's smile dimmed. "Well, hello Miss Jeanine. Can I get you anything?"

Jeanine Jones, nee Beckhoff, curled her lips as she examined Evangeline from head to toe. "How about longer trousers?"

"You're a hoot," Evangeline replied, somehow meaning it. "Can I bring you a vanilla cold brew?"

Jeanine flashed a venomous smile. Nothing was worse to Prospero's ex-wife than defeat by kindness—especially from someone she considered superior. And in Jeanine's world, looks were the only barometer. She nodded just enough to show her superiority, then folded her lean frame across Prospero.

Surgeries had been kinder to Jeanine than the years. She carried her fake boobs, Botox, and collagen lips better than the scowl etched into her soul. Long ago, Prospero had fallen in love with her smile, her bubbly demeanor, her joy at life. A lifetime ago, Jeanine had been someone else.

Until Tabitha, when their world began its collapse, when she sought solace in medication, the surgeon, and the arms of others.

"What's with the bald head?"

"I needed a change. Listen, if this is about the alimony, I can—"

She waved off the sentence. "Not here."

"Jeanine, I just…" He stopped and took a deep breath to consider his next words. "I had a rough night."

"Drinking again?"

"No." He wanted to say it was pills this time, but demurred. "Tough going with the business."

Jeanine nodded without listening. She leaned in. "Liam and I are getting married. I wanted you to be the first to know."

The words exploded in his chest. "Now?"

She nodded.

"Don't you think that's a bit rash?"

"I think a year is more than enough. I was hoping you'd be happy."

"Happy!" He leaned in and hissed. "Happy? That your college boyfriend couldn't wait until our marriage died when he pounced on you?"

"We found each other again, Pete. After you and I spent beautiful years together. It is time for new beginnings."

It had taken years for Prospero to understand how talented a manipulator Jeanine Beckhoff could be. Using her pet name for him, alluding to the past, making everything conveniently perfect so she could have her way. Pointedly ignoring the multiple affairs she justified as a salve for the pain of a stillborn daughter.

He always lost in these conversations. So he sat back, considering her, when Evangeline brought the coffee.

"Here you go, Jeanine. I brought you some half and half as well."

Perhaps Evangeline did not understand how powerful a weapon her kindness could be. If she did, she wielded it innocently, and well.

"Thank you, dear." Jeanine pursed her lips, a cornered animal. "Have you been gaining weight?"

Prospero wanted to snap at his ex-wife, at the astounding pettiness she showed around anyone she considered a threat. His friend did not need his help.

"I don't think so," Evangeline replied, twisting to consider her hips. "I just eat healthy." She smiled and sauntered off, the jab ignored with sass and grace.

"That was very mean, Jay."

"Oh please. It's disgusting. She could be your daughter. You should be ashamed."

"She is the last person who treats me like a human, Jay. And she barely knows I exist. More than I can say about you and Liam for the last stretch of our marriage."

"Oh, is that it? Now you're jealous? I try to share my happiness with you, and all you can talk about is your insecurity and failure?" Her voice rose enough to drown out every other conversation in the cafe.

"Why don't you order another coffee from your pudgy high-school crush? And then send me a note from pedophile jail after you're done being someone else's bitch."

She stood up, snatched her coffee, and walked out.

CHAPTER 5

Prospero returned his coffee cup to the counter instead of the bin by the door, which provided an opportunity for a personal apology. The cafe's video screen blared the ever-present ads for the latest model of AR glasses, and the do-it-all apps that automated every aspect of life. Escaping reality became easier with each passing day. Perhaps he should make the choice to join the rest of humanity and insulate himself from it.

"I'm so sorry about that," he said, motioning to the table under the window.

Evangeline smiled out of the corner of her eye. "I deal with this a lot. She still has feelings for you."

"Not anymore. You were exceptionally gracious, and she insulted you." He dared to look her in the eye. "And you're not gaining weight."

She shrugged and laughed. "But my shorts are probably too tight!"

He looked away and felt his cheeks flush.

"Is everything okay with you two?"

"Guess so. She told me she's getting married."

She blew out her cheeks. "Wow. That would be a little... strange."

He surprised himself with a chuckle. "That's an understatement. Lots of drama there."

"Hang in there." She paused until he looked her in the eye.

"Thank you, Evangeline. See you tomorrow."

He walked into the blooming day, smoldering with shame. Yesterday, Evangeline's aloof cordiality had been tolerable: he might be nothing in her world, but at least he was not an obstacle. Today's unrequited pity was a burden. Knowing she felt sorry for him justified every step he'd taken up to last night's decision.

He thought about asking Evangeline for help — a friendly ear, nothing more — and quickly shunted the image. He imagined the disastrous scene: knocking on her door, bawling his eyes out, sitting on her couch or futon or whatever better-smelling furniture she had, then admitting that he'd failed at everything he'd ever—

Something far away—the seething murmur of a far-off ocean—tugged at his mind. He gazed up to see an elderly woman enter the crosswalk, oblivious to a vehicle barreling her way. The driver—a kid engrossed with his handset—was texting.

Prospero tried to scream, but couldn't. The vehicle, black and shiny and enormous, barreled towards the woman, who now looked up, screaming during the last seconds of her life.

His ears roared, and time stopped. If he could move faster, or if she could come to him—

Tires screeched, the vehicle stopped, and something tugged. Prospero stared into the bleary eyes of the old woman, who gazed back in awe. The scream faded from her lips.

"What did you do?"

He was about to ask what she meant and realized the voice came from someone behind him.

"I'm sorry, what?"

"What did you just do?" A woman pointed at him, looking surprised through her AR visor. "You pulled her away! How did you do that?"

"I didn't do anything, I just—"

"You pulled her out of the street!" Another bystander lifted his visor, joining the fray. "She just flew toward you! What is going on?"

The intersection writhed with car horns, screeching tires, people getting out and pointing at the scene. The kid in the truck stared at him through a pair of trendy glasses, mouth open in shock. In the cacophony, one sentence blasted his mind.

You pulled her away.

"What happened? Everything okay?"

He turned to the familiar voice. Evangeline, flushed from sprinting to the scene, caught her breath.

"I'm... not sure. I'm not sure what happened."

"He saved me!" The old woman grabbed him, making the sign of the cross in front of his face. "Να σε καλοστένει ο Θεός. May God bless you, my child. Thank you. Ευχαριστώ."

"He pulled her off the street," a woman behind said, louder this time. "How did you do that?"

Evangeline's touch sent a shiver down his spine. "What happened, Prospero? Are you okay?"

"I'm... fine?" He stared at the old lady, still holding him; at the woman still pointing; and at the kid in the truck, slack-jawed in amazement or terror, when everything swayed.

"I have to go." He nodded at the woman, extricating

himself from her grasp, and ran away. He had no idea where. Home was too far; down Main Street too slow. So he headed south, a block from the bike path, hoping for the anonymity of the older neighborhoods surrounding downtown.

He clutched his book, sprinting without aim. For how long he could not tell. A block, maybe two, before slowing at a stop sign by the library. He looked at the sky, now rid of clouds and brilliant blue, when he felt her.

Andy Vestal stepped out of nowhere, a wide smile brightening her face.

"You believe me now?"

CHAPTER 6

Prospero gasped, trying to catch his breath after the sprint. "Believe what?"

"Believe what I told you."

"I don't know what you're talking about, Ms. Vestal. Weird shit is happening today."

"Name's Andy," she said with a laugh. "And that wasn't weird. Let's walk and I'll explain everything."

"Let's not," Prospero replied, gulping down air. "Can you tell me what the hell is happening?"

"I can tell you this isn't hell," she said with a wink. She started walking away from the fray, and despite his better judgment, Prospero followed.

The sun warmed the sidewalks, the air heavier than it had been the day before. "What just happened back there?"

"A happy accident. Or better said, a happily avoided accident."

"You didn't answer my question. A woman popped into my arms for no reason, and now everyone's pointing at me. What's going on?"

She glanced up. "What did you study, Prospero?"

"Engineering. You're not answering my question."

"If I looked at your social media history, what posts would I find?" She turned to him with a knowing arch of her eyebrows. "I'm only interested in the academic subjects. Not your frequent image searches for a certain PhD candidate, of course."

He flushed at the comment. "Math and astronomy. I'm a science geek. Jay hated that. And you're still not answering my question."

She ignored the riposte. "Do you know what the observer effect is?"

"Why are you asking me questions instead of answering mine?"

"So you don't know what the observer effect is?"

He closed his eyes and gritted his teeth. "It says that observation can affect some scientific measurements. Where are you going with this?"

"It is far more than that," she replied. "The Von Neumann–Wigner interpretation of quantum mechanics states that consciousness can change reality. "

"Oh, geez, so sorry. You want me to look that up and explain that to the old woman?"

Andy shrugged. "You're angry at things you can't explain. I'm trying to help you understand."

He stopped on the sidewalk to laugh. "Okay, this is ridiculous. I'm walking with a woman who broke into my apartment after I tried to kill myself, and now you're quizzing me on quantum mechanics and it is somehow my fault?"

He shook his head with a derisive snort. "I've had enough. Goodbye, Andy Vestal—if that's your real name."

He turned to leave, headed to the coffee shop, unsure of

anything except wanting to see Evangeline, and tell her he was going insane.

Turn around, Prospero.

The words roared into his mind, a pressure more than a sound. He turned to find Andy smiling.

"What are you doing to me?"

"Sharing a secret."

He stepped closer, shaken. "Tell me what the hell is going on. *Now.*"

She tilted her head and gazed at him with a placid smile. "Like I said. This isn't hell."

"Stop it!" He turned to face her and pointed a finger at her face. "I'm at the bottom of my life, Andy. I'm broke, my career failed, and I can't pay alimony. My ex-wife conned me into adopting kids I don't know, and today she informed me she's getting married to the guy she cheated with throughout our marriage. And I can't even kill myself properly."

"Well, then. I'll tell you: you've been chosen to save consciousness itself."

The low rumble started deep, turning into a spasm, and he burst out laughing.

"Oh, holy shit, that is awesome. Wow." He wiped his eyes and shook his head. "Gotta give it to you, Andy. You had me going for a while there. All the science stuff you vomited out was pretty impressive. Whoever the hell you are, and whatever trick you're playing, that was well done. But I'm not donating."

"Donating to what?"

"To whatever bullshit new-age church you belong to. Goodbye."

"I don't belong to a church, Prospero." Andy's expression didn't change. "Order is permanence. Once it arises, it doesn't disappear—it changes everything around it. And consciousness is the highest form of order, the universe becoming aware of itself. Your fate is to save it."

"You sound like someone dumped a load of metaphysical posters into a hamster wheel."

"Hadn't considered that," she replied with a nod and a smile. "One more question?"

"Please just go away. Leave me alone."

"Where do we go when we die?"

"You are a lunatic." He shook his head and walked away—until she called after him.

"Why are you so enamored of Evangeline See?"

The question froze him. He turned toward her with a snarl. "I'm *not enamored* of her."

"Of course, of course. Why?"

He glanced around them, ensuring privacy, before answering. "That's personal."

"You follow her online. Quite avidly, I might add. And you spend a lot of time at the coffee shop when she's there. Why?"

He wanted to answer *That's none of your damn business*, but Evangeline was his favorite topic. "She's... different. Real. She doesn't numb herself with tech. She's, I don't know. Alive? Look around you."

He gestured to the street. Around them, stuck in various traps of technology, people droned through a world with which they did not interact. Across the street, a mother chatted into the air like a madman, having an invisible conversation with someone through her glasses. Her child gazed at the sky, filtering the world through an AR visor designed for tiny faces, a marketing ploy Prospero considered profane. Beyond that, a couple walked next to each other, not touching, each consumed by whatever their handsets and earphones fed them. None had any desire to interact with the world. Or perhaps they'd lost the will to do so.

Andy's voice softened. "I want you to remember that."

"Remember what?"

"That clarity. Her awareness. That choice."

She walked away, turned a corner, and vanished.

Prospero stayed, searching for a one-liner to shout at her, remaining silent instead.

Then, he heard her.

"Who the heck is she?"

Evangeline yelled at him from across the street, sunlight shimmering in her hair. He was wishing for the light to turn green when it did, and a faded blue minivan screeched to a stop as she ran across to him.

"Who was that?"

He shook his head, avoiding her gaze. "Someone from work. Strange day."

"That kid in the truck said you pulled that old lady off the street."

He shrugged. "I don't think he saw anything. He was texting."

"Two other women said the same thing." She gulped a lungful of air to calm her breath.

"I don't think they were paying attention."

"The old lady said you snatched her from the crosswalk." She crossed her arms and shook her head. "What's going on?"

"Evangeline, I have no idea what's going on. But I'd love to buy you a drink sometime and try to explain." He winced, immediately regretting the comment.

She'd never looked at him this way. "Did you say 'buy me a drink'?"

"I don't mean anything bad by it; I just need someone to talk to. A friend."

She was silent for an eternity, enough for Prospero to wish he could crawl underground, when she blossomed into a smile.

"Are you... asking me out?"

"I would really like to talk to you. If that's okay."

She raised her chin and considered him through narrowed eyes. "You around tomorrow?"

"I'm always around." He felt naked, terrified, and alive.

"Happy hour at Bobby's? I get off at five." She turned with a wave, and for the first time in too long, Prospero Jones felt hope.

CHAPTER 7

The walk to his apartment passed in a crash of memories. He crossed the street he'd walked hours before, steps that almost became the last evidence of his life on earth.

Was this a convoluted dream? Waking up after falling asleep in the water, finding a stranger in his bedroom; fantastic episodes with his clothes and the car and Andy's voice in his mind? Maybe all of this was an illusion, a reaction to the pills. Either a dream or a hallucination, or both.

He stepped into the corner liquor store, nodding at the strung-out cashier. A dozen QR codes for new beer, all-in-one social media apps, and habanero-flavored tequila covered every surface. Being one of two people who did not own AR glasses — Evangeline being the only other—he'd miss the ever-present advertisements anchored to the ubiquitous black and white squares where the virtual world intersected with the real. Despite the lack of digital cartography, he found the rum aisle a mere twenty feet inside the store. He picked up a bland bottle—no doubt a stunner through the right glasses— and felt his stomach drop.

Drinking alone would be defeat.

He left without buying anything and kept walking home.

Houses set back from streets paved with red brick boasted brilliant green plants overflowing their pots in early spring glory. The tang of oxygen diffusing from them tasted different from the aroma of trees and grass. Shimmering heat emanated at different rates from earth to concrete, roiling into the sky, leaving lazy vortices of—

He stopped. Had he ever noticed *any* of that before? Was this a dream, or was he going mad? Invisible things he knew were there, reachable only by analysis and imagination, were now as real to him as the ground beneath his feet.

He glanced around him, aware of everything. The pulsing of far-off noise borne on the wind, the tickle of radio waves somewhere inside his skull, the scattering of blue and ultraviolet from the deep sky. Everything around him intertwined with everything else; every connection knowable, discoverable, and malleable.

He picked up a pebble from beneath a tidy planter, a fragment of limestone rising from the beach soil. Everything around here was the same: ancient rocks deposited from a receding sea millions of years ago. He squeezed, thinking of Andy's comment on the forces of nature.

Could this be real? He tugged the jacket he'd worn last night, bone dry after whatever he'd done in his sink.

He squeezed the pebble, thinking of what else was possible, when an image of the hills of Tennessee — a trip taken before he knew his marriage was breaking—slipped into his mind. Everything around glowed in his mind, and his ears popped, as if stifling a yawn.

Cold radiated from the masonry planter by his arm. But

cold didn't radiate, he knew: heat flowed out. Why was the structure so cold? Where did the energy escape?

He felt the warmth in his hand and noticed the limestone was gone. In its place, a grainy, translucent chunk of marble glinted dull in the sunlight.

How he knew all of this, he couldn't say. Images and knowledge appeared, guiding control of something he did not understand. He poked at the fragment in his hand, his breath catching is ragged gasps. When he touched the planter, he recoiled in surprise. The concrete and stone had chilled below freezing, an impossibility in the warming day.

Something dropped in his stomach as he held the fragment, imagining particles flying into the void. Unseen structure raced across his mind with clear understanding, order within chaos.

He dropped the rock when it became too hot to hold.

"Oh, no, no, no..."

He tried to swallow and failed. The chunk glowed a color he somehow knew only he could see. Atomic decay, the cause of the radioactivity, lay bare on the gray sidewalks of Mullet Cove.

He'd crafted something radioactive. Uranium? Who cared? Some kid playing with the pebble might burn herself, or maybe he'd blow up the block, or...

He squeezed his eyes to focus, forcing a very specific image into his mind. Specks of light and energy turning to matter, coalescing into heavier, more stable things. For yards beyond him, the sidewalk buckled as heat flowed into the pebble, leaving dry, frozen concrete in its wake. All of this happened at his command, unimaginable and impossible, as if a million voices whispered in his mind and showed him how.

Whatever he was doing, he'd better not screw up.

A loud pop, then silence.

He opened one eye, expecting destruction. A thin cloud of dust hung low over the pebble, then scurried away, borne by a soft breeze. Prospero bent low to examine the source. The fragment of radioactive metal had disappeared, replaced by a dull, heavy lump.

Lead.

CHAPTER 8

He sat alone at Bobby's bar, sipping a warm beer, and turning the sliver of metal in his hands. The dull surface caught the light of a lazy afternoon.

It shouldn't have been this heavy. He'd picked up a chunk of limestone, changed it into something harmless, warped it into something lethal, and ended up with something dense, heavy, and unnatural.

How the hell did this happen?

It wasn't lead after all, but bismuth, an element he had forgotten from high school, yet now, for some inexplicable reason, he could name. The certainty of it sat in his mind like an intrusive dream, a memory he hadn't sought but understood.

He traced the condensation under the beer bottle, noticing for the first time how much his ears had been ringing. Was it high blood pressure? Maybe he was just attuned to something, and the numbness was how it felt to slip into an awareness he did not understand.

But most likely, he was just losing his mind.

The old woman in the street; the way the world had slowed when it should have surged forward; the metal in his palm. None of this made sense. Maybe it was all a delirious spell caused by stress, the years of scraping by, the failed businesses, the fall into irrelevance, and ultimately into nothing. Maybe he needed to go to the doctor, get some bloodwork done, and get his vitals checked.

Or maybe it was because last night, he'd tried to kill himself, and failed. Near-death experiences rewired the brain, he'd once read. They caused hallucinations, delusions, and a shifting sense of reality. Maybe he was already gone, and this was one banger of a dream.

But none of this felt like a delusion. It felt more real than anything had in years. And dreams were messy, not a specific rewrite of the laws of heat transfer, turning sidewalk frost into metal.

Not sober dreams, anyway.

He ripped his eyes away from the beer coaster. Tomorrow, he'd sit at this very bar, with Bobby watching over him, and tell Evangeline everything: that he was unraveling, that something had shifted inside him, that he was going insane.

And maybe, that she was the only person who might help him.

He scoffed at the thought. Evangeline would respond like an angel. She'd laugh, and maybe listen, and pat his forearm and tell him everything would work out. That's what she managed with everyone. Even in her lowest moments, she was a light in everyone's life.

More than likely, she'd see him for what he was: an unraveling lunatic, spiraling ever down, and walk away from him, for good.

"You always let your drinks go warm?"

Andy's voice cut through his thoughts. She sat across the corner of the bar, hands folded, watching him with a placid gaze. Had she been there the whole time? Did she just appear whenever she damn well pleased?

He exhaled, blowing out his cheeks. "You again."

She nodded, almost amused. "Me again."

He picked up his beer and took a slow sip. Andy didn't move, didn't glance around, didn't fidget. She didn't even pretend to belong here. Bobby approached, asking if she needed something. She thanked him with a kind smile, as if he were an extra in a movie.

"Are you stalking me?"

"No. Just checking in," she said, like she hadn't turned his world inside out.

Prospero set the bottle down with more force than necessary. "I was doing just fine without your bullshit. Now I'm nursing a beer wondering if I need to check myself into a hospital." He slipped the metal into his coat pocket. "Can you please just leave me alone?"

Andy tilted her head, eyes flickering with something almost human. "Sorry for dumping all of this on you. It's a lot."

Prospero let out a silent chuckle. "A lot? I feel like I lost my mind somewhere between the bridge and this damn bar." He signaled to Bobby for another round. "But maybe I'm sane, and you're just a con artist."

He'd only known her for a few hours, but in that time, he'd clocked several of her emotions. This one was the placid, maddening smile, the one she used to stump him.

"I don't need you to believe me," she said. "I just want you to ask the right questions."

Then she stood up and left.

He wanted to yell *No, I won't* after her, but that would've seemed desperate, even for him. And if he was going to meet Evangeline tomorrow night, creating a scene with this strange woman wasn't the wisest of choices.

But beyond that, he thought *maybe she was right.*

Right now, he was just tired. He paid his tab, waved to Bobby, and left.

Andy was nowhere in sight. Main Street was dying down, the last vestiges of meeting groups or clubs or surreptitious encounters ending and going home. He turned towards the coast and walked. Past the bayou, past the mansions that flooded with every high tide, until he reached his neglected apartment complex, with its concrete walls and forgotten dreams.

He fumbled his way inside, brushed his teeth under the light of a flickering bulb, and stared at the ceiling, wondering if he was going mad.

That night, he dreamed of Tabitha.

The next morning, he kept his eyes closed for a long time, trying to keep the dream from evanescing. Normally he couldn't remember dreams, but this one was vivid as life: Tabitha running barefoot through the home she'd never seen, into a forest she'd only known from inside Jeanine's belly. Her laughter rang like delicate bells, and her golden hair sparkled in the fading light. She ran up to him and stared with clear, honeyed eyes—Jeanine's eyes—then asked him a nightmare question.

"What happens when we fall asleep, Daddy?"

His throat tightened, even in the light of day. "I don't know, sweetheart," he'd told her in the dream. "But when you wake up, I'll be here."

She'd smiled, bright and beautiful and warm, and when

he woke up, she was gone. He could not remember Tabitha's face. But it had been her, the first time he'd dreamed of her since she'd died inside Jeanine.

Pale morning light filtered through the filthy window. Dust lingered in the air, floating in slow, silent specks. He dressed deep in thought, remembering Andy's admonition about clean dishes. Her trick now seemed obvious: she'd turned organic crap from his dirty dishes into methane, carbon dioxide, and ammonia. How she could do that he did not yet know. He remembered the chill on his feet as she walked out, the same hard frost on the planter when he transmuted limestone into something else, the chill of his sink when he dried his clothes. The energy to change atoms needed to come from somewhere, and heat surrounded them.

So he decided on an experiment to spite her: clean windows.

He tried Andy's technique, but nothing happened. He unearthed a forgotten footstool and tried the old-fashioned way: wiping the mix of grease and dirt and salt with a rag, then a brush.

Nothing except streaks of grease and dirt.

"What the hell were you thinking?" he mumbled to himself. "That you can harness energy?"

He shook his head and murmured a repeated mantra—*You are an idiot*—under his breath.

He changed out his clothes and stepped outside. The apartment reminded him too much of defeat, and most of the time he wished to be anywhere else. Before closing the door, he glanced back and felt empty.

The grime on his windows was evidence—and symptom —of his defeat. For a soul bent on self-destruction, the feeble light of a summer morning represented hope. And he couldn't even enjoy it. Because he was a pathetic loser, and a slob.

He'd fallen so far. His anger at his choices had consumed him, and somewhere along that descent he'd forgotten to live. Prospero Jones clung to his failures like a castaway groping for the ship he knew would doom him. Would Tabitha have been embarrassed by her father?

So he walked back in, slammed the door behind him and focused on the dust and grime with all his might. No use hiding the fact that minutes ago he'd tried and failed. In his mind, this time the dust evanesced into simple compounds, scattering in the air. He narrowed his eyes and focused so hard that his ears rang with a hollow throb.

Seconds later, he had to stare away and back from the window to see the change. The dust and grime must've sublimed into organics, if the smell was any indication. The process—he hoped he hadn't created alien DNA—took so much heat that the central air shut off in the middle of a Gulf Coast morning.

He somehow knew the building absorbed a lot more energy in the infrared. The dark concrete outside would be teeming with heat energy. He focused on another window-pane, bridging the gap between source and target. The grime evanesced into the warming day as the glass turned clear before his stupefied eyes.

His ears rang as he realized he had no idea what the hell he was doing. But cleaning house—and his windows—had become a lot easier.

CHAPTER 9

For the second day in a row, Prospero sat at the corner of Bobby's, this time nursing a club soda. The video screen behind the bar droned away with bullshit ads peddling AR glasses, dorky-looking visors, apps promising escape, and the latest mysterious new product release. The end of thought, he mused, arrived with significant discounts—but only if you purchased now.

Forty hours had passed since he'd tried to kill himself. Almost thirty since he'd performed alchemy on a cracked sidewalk in a forgotten town in Florida. Twelve or so since an unforgettable dream about his dead daughter. A little less since he'd cleaned his apartment using nothing but the heat emanating from his apartment building's walls. His temples throbbed with the dull roar of a stifled yawn.

He played with the rosy sliver of bismuth, then stuffed it back into his pocket. No need to flaunt evidence among the sparse patrons this early on a weekday afternoon. The metal somehow grounded him, proof that despite the impossibility of the last days, what was happening was *real*.

The video cut from sports highlights to a pair of talking heads, both looking ridiculous in the latest version of augmented reality glasses. Apex Industries, the behemoth monopoly that cornered the entire digital market, would soon open a huge data center a dozen miles inland from Mullet Cove. The bastards had leveled a forest to build another unnecessary building. Prospero hoped the traffic wouldn't screw up what was left of the little town.

Bobby had muted the screen, a helpful gesture to the patrons, so Prospero followed the thinly veiled ad by reading lips. The Apex CEO, a trim guy in his fifties with too much hair and not enough wrinkles, forced a bored smile for the camera. The glasses his company sold by the millions did not perch on *his* face. Maybe that had provided him with enough attention span to grow a business empire, one that had built a supersonic transport, an underground highway, and various models of autonomous cars. Every single breakthrough integrated seamlessly with the company's phones and glasses, allowing people to travel across continents and never take their eyes off the manufactured crap injected into their eyes.

He took a long sip of soda and let out a low, sour chuckle. Even in this shithole, he'd rather be looking outside the entire time.

"Hey, you!"

Evangeline stepped out of the afternoon light into the cool darkness of the bar. He felt a shiver of guilt recalling Jay's opinion of the length of her shorts.

"Hey." He patted the stool near him. "Saved a spot for you."

They sat at the corner of the bar, across from the one where he'd seen Andy last night. He faced Evangeline across the corner to make sure he didn't make her uncomfortable.

Bobby greeted her with a vague nod. "Hey Eve. Whatcha having?"

"Hey. How about a house red?"

"Two?" Bobby asked, and Prospero nodded.

She leaned her chin on her hand and flicked her hair over her shoulder. "You okay?"

He wanted to tell her everything. "I'm good. Thanks for coming."

She narrowed her eyes and hinted at a smile. "Something's off. Are you losing weight?"

He chuckled. "That's way nicer than what Jeanine said."

She rolled her eyes in assent. "So are you getting ready to go back to dating?"

He laughed and shook his head. "I'm too old for that, Evangeline."

"Stop it! You keep saying that, but you don't act like it. Are you going to grow your hair back?"

"I'm not sure."

She pursed her lips in a wry frown. "I'd like to see you rocking a buzz cut. I think it would look really nice."

"That's the nicest thing anyone's ever said about my hair."

They chatted about everything. Bobby hooked them up with house cabs well past the end of happy hour, and Prospero remembered how easy it felt to smile.

"Let me get this straight. You finished your PhD coursework up north, decided to stop, came here without a job, and now you're..."

"Making coffee? My, someone's very judgmental tonight."

"I didn't mean that."

She shrugged. "It's okay. One day I realized I'd know exactly what I'd be doing next year, and the one after that. One decision that would spawn a life I could not imagine. I wanted a life where I had to live for today, where the decisions were mine alone."

"Wise beyond your years, Evangeline."

She pushed his arm in jest. "Stop acting so old. You're not much older than me."

"I could be your father." The words punched him in the gut.

"You're terrible at math. Not unless you had me when you were, what? Twelve?"

"Not sure how to take that."

Her eyes drilled into his soul. "I'll be thirty soon. Can you believe that? I never imagined this is what it would feel like."

"You're at the height of your superpowers. I, however, am on the other side of forty."

"Stop it. You could be my older brother. And more importantly, you don't act old. You're just... normal." She tilted her head and stared into his soul. "In a nice way."

He was about to reply with something self-deprecating when someone burst through the door. The young man glanced around for an instant, checking out the bar through his very trendy glasses, before his gaze fell on Evangeline. He carried the impatience of someone at his physical peak, whose wisdom had yet to develop, and whose anger had yet to cool.

"Yo, Eve! Where've you been?"

She flashed a wan smile. "Hello, Luke."

Prospero captured the full weight of the disdain in her brief gesture. Luke, looking at the world through the filters on his glasses, did not. He plopped onto a barstool next to Evangeline, ignoring everyone else.

"How come you're not returning my texts?"

"Because I don't use a smartphone. By the way, this is my friend from work, Prospero."

Luke ignored Prospero with a "yeah" before he could even respond. "What about the one I gave you?"

"You mean the leash?" Evangeline replied. "I'm not gonna be tied to a phone, Luke."

"It's the twenty-first century, Eve. C'mon. It was really expensive."

"How about calling or visiting the shop?"

"I got you a very nice smartphone as a gift. Not everyone gets something like that."

"That was very sweet, Luke. But we're not dating. And you know that wasn't a gift."

Luke rolled his eyes. "Do you ever stop with the tech purist act? Any other chick would be very appreciative of what I did for you. A lot of women want to be treated like that."

Evangeline looked away. She locked eyes with Prospero for a momentary, exasperated glare.

"Don't look away when I'm talking to you."

"I thought you were done talking about phones."

He grabbed her wrist and pulled her toward him. "Don't you disrespect me. I'm trying to be nice."

Evangeline needed no help from the assembled group. She ripped his hand away and pushed Luke off the stool. "Don't you *ever* touch me again, do you understand?"

"Whoa! Who the fuck do you think you are?"

Bobby the bartender slapped down a cleaning rag. "Hey Vandemere, knock it off or leave."

"This is personal, asshole." He glared at Evangeline. "If you're not using that phone, I want it back. I'm not spending money on you for nothing."

"You thought you could *buy me* with a damn phone?" She bared her teeth at him. "That is offensive and pathetic."

Luke stepped too close. "Do you have any idea who you're talking to?"

"Someone who needs to pay money to get laid?"

Luke raised his hand, and something burst in Prospero's mind.

"Don't you dare touch her."

Luke stopped. "Shut the fuck up, old man."

"Leave her alone."

Evangeline glanced over her shoulder. "Thank you, but you don't have to do this."

"Leave her alone, Luke. Please."

"You want to be brave in front of your granddaughter?" Luke pointed an angry fist. "I'll show you how to be brave. Outside, asshole. Now."

"Luke, stop with the macho shit, will you? And you wonder why I'm not interested."

"Shut up, Eve. Old man, get your pussy ass outside. I'm going to teach you a fucking lesson."

Decades ago, Prospero would've felt alive at the challenge. One day ago, his insides would've soured at the threat, the bluster, the anticipation of pain. His physical peak was behind him, and soon he would find out by how much.

But today he sipped the last of his wine, slapped a few bills on the counter, and stood up. Everything had changed.

"Be right back, Bobby," Prospero said with a smile, and stepped into the night.

CHAPTER 10

A thin fringe of orange clung to the western sky as the remnants of early spring heat emanated from the surrounding concrete. Prospero walked south, well past the bar windows, almost reaching Main Street. The owner of the corner shop had painted colorful wings at shoulder height, Mullet Cove's most popular spot for teenage photos. The concrete, still warm to the touch, reached uninterrupted to the building's roof. Oceans of energy around him, ready to be formed.

He turned to face Luke and smiled.

"You're pretty fucking dumb to try to be a hero, old man. Don't tell me you're trying to fuck her."

Prospero chuckled and shook his head. "Not at all. She—"

He looked up from the ground, his face full and wet. Luke stood above him, lips curled in disdain.

"You can't even take a punch, pussy. You didn't even see that coming." He coughed something and spat on him.

"Luke, you asshole! What did you do to him?"

"Stay back, Eve. And you..." Luke knelt beside him. "Get

the fuck up and fight, or stay down like the little bitch you are."

His heart raced. Fear of pain and disfigurement and shame consumed him. Far beyond, Evangeline stood by the bar entrance, yelling something unintelligible. Bobby the bartender muttered something into a phone.

The police would be here soon. He didn't need to be helped, treated like a victim, and shamed.

Not in front of Evangeline.

He propped up on the warm sidewalk, feeling the heat deep inside the concrete and rock and earth.

Luke stood up and shook his head in disdain. "I knew it. You're a fucking loser. Stay out of my business next time."

The heat roiled around him, strings pulled by thought. Then the sidewalk chilled, spidering frost onto the painted wings on the pale blue wall. The heat, pulled and formed by his mind, coiled like a serpent, a vast machine.

Then Prospero let it go.

Luke took one step towards Evangeline, then stiffened. He teetered, then fell, stiff as a board, smashing face-first into the sidewalk with a hollow crack. In moments, blood pooled from his open mouth, carrying bits of something white. Teeth?

A trooper raced across the street, eyes darting between Prospero and Luke.

"I'm fine," Prospero said, and sat up. "I don't think he is."

A few minutes later he sat at the bar, holding a leaky bag of ice over his eye. The red and blue lights of an ambulance pulsed through the bar windows, reflecting over bottles and polished taps. Evangeline walked in, and his heart lurched.

"What happened to him?"

"EMT said it was a seizure. Pretty bad one."

"Is he going to be okay?"

"Why are you asking about him?" Evangeline looked at him with a curious pout. "He *hit* you, Prospero. He *assaulted* you. I gave the police a statement. Bobby's talking to them now."

"I'll recover. Looked like he lost some teeth."

She blew out her cheeks. "He was out. Broke his nose, and his fancy glasses shredded half of his face. Lucky he didn't lose an eye. Never seen anything like that." She pulled the bag away from his face and winced. "He deserves it for being such an asshole. And you're going to have a heck of a shiner."

"Kind of embarrassing at my age."

She pulled the bag off and once again stared into his soul. "That was very brave, Prospero. Reckless and unnecessary and brave. I guess chivalry isn't dead. Especially among knuckle-heads like you."

She smiled. When she touched his face, all pain evaporated.

He stalled for words, wondering if she'd ever find out. "I didn't like what he said to you." He placed the bag over his eye. "Did he really buy you a phone so you'd go out with him?"

Evangeline smirked. "I think he wanted to bypass the whole... courting thing."

He stared back, slack-jawed. "He bought you a phone so you'd sleep with him?"

She raised her eyebrows and nodded, surprised he didn't know.

"Geez, Evangeline. Is that what the kids are doing these days?"

"The end of romance, I guess." She rested her chin on her hands and shrugged. "And people wonder why I have a flip phone and no glasses, why I read paperbacks, and love taking photos with film cameras." She pointed at a silent ad interrupting a college basketball game, the relentless blather of more digital tools to escape life. "Everyone complains about the world, and yet we still race to hand off our lives online. I guess I miss the old days."

"Did you..."

"Did I what?"

"You know... the phone."

She pushed him away in jest. "No! Are you serious? You think I'd fall for someone like that?"

"No," he said, and shook his head in relief. "Listen, I know this is none of my business, but you deserve someone far better." Outside, Bobby the bartender related the tale to the police officer, gesturing at the ambulance. "You're very special, Evangeline. A treasure different from anyone else. You have a beautiful soul and deserve far better than you receive. I hope someday you find someone who understands how incredible you are. Not some asshole like that."

She stared at him for an uncomfortable length of time. "Why are you telling me this?"

"Because someone has to. Sorry if I was too blunt."

She blossomed into a soft smile and was about to speak when Bobby burst through the door.

"Hey man, are you okay?"

Prospero nodded. "I am. Thanks for the help."

"It's nothing. Tab's on me tonight."

"You don't have to—"

He raised a hand. "I should've thrown that asshole out as soon as he touched her. I'm really sorry, Eve."

"Hey." She hugged Bobby and nodded. "Thanks."

"You guys need another round?"

Prospero shook his head and tapped the bills still on the sticky bar. "For next time."

Bobby weaved his way behind the bar and pushed the money back. "Your money's no good tonight. You won't be paying for a while, buddy. That was fuckin' ballsy. Stupid, but ballsy."

Prospero pulled the ice off and blinked. "How do I look?"

Evangeline wrinkled her nose. "You look like crap."

"I should go home. Enough fun for one night." He slipped off the bar, stuffed the bills in the tip jar, and nodded at them. "See you all later."

Evangeline watched him leave without a word. Prospero stepped into the cool night and walked past the spot where, moments ago, he'd almost killed a man.

Tonight, he'd done something he could not explain. He was an idiot and a dreamer and a loser, but hope sparked through the swirl of despair that had become the backdrop of his life.

Andy Vestal, whoever the heck she was, was not a con artist. Prospero had no idea who she was, but he'd find out. What mattered most now was understanding what was happening to him. And why?

He turned right on Main Street, heading home. The brass fittings on the wooden doors of the coffee shop glinted in the night. He wondered if he'd ever return, if he'd ever dare to see Evangeline again after tonight's embarrassment.

In another life, a better one, he would've met her first. But that fantasy lay in madness. What Prospero Jones needed was to stop time, to wait out the clock, to be closer in age to the one person left on this planet who made life worth living.

But no amount of bending heat into electric shock, or turning limestone to bismuth, or drying clothes by sublimating water would ever make that happen. He was alone and would be for the rest of his life. It was high time he got used to the condition.

Before he reached the crosswalk, he heard her voice.

"You need someone to help you with that shiner," Evangeline said with a smile. "Come on."

CHAPTER 11

"Ouch."

"I'm sorry!" Evangeline said and leaned back. "Did I hurt you?"

"Just a little sting."

She bit her lip in concentration. "I'm almost done."

Prospero sat in Evangeline's tiny kitchen as she cleaned a cut on his eyebrow. After several glasses of wine and a lot of laughing, Evangeline had bolted upright and attacked him with a paper towel. A small cut, barely scabbed over from the ice bag in the bar, had split open, bleeding all over his face. Evangeline set up a makeshift first aid station in her kitchen and insisted on fixing him up.

"Okay, it's pretty clean. I'm going to put a butterfly stitch on it."

"How many glasses of wine have you had?"

"Including this afternoon?" She glanced off to the side and shrugged. "Six. Maybe seven?"

"You fill me with confidence, Doctor See."

She stuck out her tongue and giggled. "You are a terrible patient, you know that?"

He had great difficulty looking away as Evangeline tended to his cut. Her blouse, loose and airy for the cafe, was not designed for up-close first aid. Evangeline took her sweet time ensuring his cut was cleaned just so, and the view just right. He didn't mind the attention.

She placed the bandage over his eyebrow, kissed her finger, and touched it to his nose. "I hope you get better."

"Thank you. I feel great already."

They put away her first-aid kit — everything had come from a junk drawer in her kitchen—and she refilled their glasses.

"Are you going to bleed all over my couch again?"

"I'll sit over here if you want."

"Nope." She handed him a glass, pushed him onto the couch, and curled up facing him. She stared in silence for a long while.

"How come we've never done this before?"

"First aid in your kitchen?"

She pushed him away and bit her lip. "Talking! About everything."

"Coffee shop isn't the place, I guess. I've really enjoyed this."

"So have I." She sipped her wine and regarded him out of the corner of her eye. "I always felt so comfortable around you."

"And I feel like I've known you my whole life."

She gathered her hair over one shoulder, caressing it as she smiled. "You're different from everyone else. You are so considerate. I always think it's so sweet when you step back when it gets crazy at the shop. It's like you care."

"I do care. Because you are different from anyone else, Evangeline. You are kind, and confident, and make everyone happy."

She waved off the comment. "I don't think so..."

"You do. You're a beacon. The light of that place. And really, everywhere you go."

"You are very sweet." She squeezed his hand and ran a thumb over his knuckles. "I try to be beautiful on the inside, you know?"

"I do. It's kind of unfair."

She wrinkled her brow in a smile. "What do you mean?"

"I don't mean to make this uncomfortable, but... you're also gorgeous on the outside. Which sometimes makes talking with you very difficult."

She sat up. "You don't have to say that."

He sat up in response. "I'm sorry. I guess that was very inappropriate."

"No, it wasn't. Just...don't lie to me. Please."

He shook his head and laughed. "Lie to you? Every person who walks into that coffee shop is smitten with you."

Honey locks cascaded over her face as she shook her head. "No, they're not. I've always been *that girl*. 'Cute but plain.' I'm the sidekick."

He stared at her with a slack-jawed smile. "You cannot be serious."

"Oh, c'mon. Have you ever met Angie? Our manager?"

"I think I have."

"You *think* you have?" She pushed him again. "Guys come in just to stare at her. She's tiny and cute. Not me." She wrinkled her nose. "Look at me. I'm not skinny and bubbly. I have big eyebrows. And hips. And my teeth are too big." She bared her canines in a growl, then burst into laughter.

"I think you have perfect teeth."

She almost snorted out her wine. "That is the most romantic thing anyone's ever told me!"

He shifted to face her. "Please don't take this the wrong way. The first time I saw you, I couldn't speak."

She stopped laughing and sat back, touching her neck.

"You are... stunning. I wish I had better words. I want to learn another language just so I can describe your eyes. You glow when you smile. Your simplest movement is like watching ballet. When you walk up the steps to the loft, or clean a table, or wave at a customer, I'm floored by the life in you, a spark that no one else has. And then you offer a kind word to someone you've never met, and frankly..."

Her eyes sparkled in the candlelight.

"I think you're the most beautiful person who's ever lived. I'm thankful that of all the lifetimes available, I was fortunate to be in yours."

Soft silence engulfed them. He took a sip of wine and smiled. "I'm sorry. That was a bit too much."

That's when Evangeline kissed him, and everything went white.

CHAPTER 12

"Could this have waited until the morning?"

Prospero stopped to adjust his shoes — his socks were all twisted — and raced to catch up to Andy. The sound of his boots echoed in the empty night air.

"Seems like you've accomplished a lot in only one day."

"What the hell is that supposed to mean?"

"Nothing. Sleeping with a damsel in distress?"

"Do I detect some jealousy?"

She shook her head and smiled. "No. That was joy."

"What did you do to her?"

"I let her sleep off her bottles of wine. How are you faring?"

Surprisingly good, Prospero wanted to reply, after an unforgettable night. He'd wanted nothing more than to wake up next to Evangeline, sharing a hangover after the most memorable evening of his life. He'd forgotten how it felt to be with someone who meant everything.

Their first time was desperate. Evangeline, her hair cascading on his shoulders, gasped an apology for her hunger.

They opened her futon couch and bundled up, hiding from the world. The second time — had there ever been a second time with Jeanine?—was a slow exploration that Prospero would remember for as long as he lived. He fell asleep to Evangeline's thick, sweet scent, to the weight of her perfection on his skin. They slept, entwined and exhausted, in the afterglow of consumed lust.

Until Andy Vestal shook him awake and pulled him away.

He dressed quickly and quietly, marveling at the way the sheets enveloped her curves. Evangeline slept in angelic slumber. He left a note, a poem apologizing for the departure, before Andy pulled him away.

"She didn't wake up when we left. Is she okay?"

"We have much to do, Prospero." Andy turned to walk. "Keep up."

He stopped and waited until she noticed him. "You didn't answer my question. Is she okay?"

Andy turned and sighed. "She's fine, given that you two put away a couple of bottles of wine. She'll wake up after a deep sleep and reminisce about an amazing night. Now let's go."

He caught up, and they walked on.

She examined him out of the corner of her eye. "By the way, how are you feeling?"

"I'm fine."

"Headache?"

Prospero shook his head. "You still haven't told me what is going on. How you did that. And why we never take a cab."

"We're getting you ready for some important meetings."

"I thought we were saving the world. Or something like that."

She glanced at him with a sneer. "Both need better clothes than that. Tell me you still own a suit."

"Hopefully, it's still in fashion. Do I need to wear a tie?"

"You ask very curious questions, Prospero Jones. Of course not."

"Transmutation and telepathy are one thing. Double Windsor is another."

Andy Vestal responded with a laugh, a sound Prospero never expected to hear.

They arrived at his apartment as pink sunbeams bled into the eastern sky. He felt neither tired nor sleepy. Was it the walk? The night with Evangeline?

"Well, well." Andy wiped a finger on his kitchen counter. "Someone's been tidying up. Expecting a date?"

Prospero shut the door behind them, hoping no one had seen them. One day ago, having his neighbors see him with an attractive woman would've been desirable. After last night, it felt like cheating.

"I tried your trick on the dishes."

"How'd that turn out?"

"Fine until the apartment got too cold."

Andy stopped examining his possessions and turned to him. "Cold?"

"Had to pull the energy from somewhere. I tried the floor first."

"The floor?"

"Yep. Then I cleaned the windows. Took me a while to figure out how to use the heat from sunlight warming the bricks outside." He pinched the bridge of his nose and shook his head. "I can't believe I'm telling you this."

Andy nodded as she examined the panes. "What happened last night? Before your date."

He remembered Evangeline's eyes and felt his cheeks blush. "Got into a fight."

"What happened?"

He looked away. "Nothing. Some dude who was trying to get into Evangeline's pants punched me."

Andy stepped close and examined his face.

"Where?"

"Right here. He pointed at the butterfly bandage stuck to his brow. Andy examined it, then ripped it off.

"Ow! What the heck was that?"

"Seems like it's healed quite well. What happened next?"

He touched his eyebrow. The cut seemed to have closed overnight. "I, uh, shocked him."

"How?"

He shrugged. "I used heat. From the street."

Andy crossed her arms and raised an eyebrow.

"I used it to build up a charge and aimed it at him. But I didn't hurt him. I could kind of see his nerves."

Andy Vestal had limited facial expressions. Prospero had seen them all except for this one. If he had to describe it, he'd qualify it as fear.

"You changed heat energy into electricity." This was a statement, not a question.

"I didn't change it, really. You know, 'can't be created nor destroyed' kind of thing. I collected it and... let it go."

"Aimed it."

"Yeah."

"Who taught you that?"

"You didn't!" He laughed, but Andy did not. "It... made sense. I don't have to think about the details. Only the outcome. And check this out."

He placed the sliver of bismuth in her hand.

"Where did this come from?"

"A planter close to downtown. Started off as a chunk of limestone. Somehow, I made it end up like this. After making it radioactive."

Andy rolled the metal between her fingers, then returned it. "This is faster than we expected," she said under her breath.

"Who is 'we'?"

Andy raised a hand. "You still cleaning your own dishes?"

"It's only been a day."

She opened the tap on the sink to a trickle. "Can you move that stream of water?"

"I could do that with a comb, if either of us had any hair. Middle school science, you know?"

"I want you to move it with your mind."

He exhaled and focused on the stream. For a second, nothing happened. Then the thin stream bent, then twisted, then flowed up, and evanesced into a cloud of steam.

"Oops," he said, and turned off the water.

Andy tapped her fingers on the counter. "Let me see that suit."

CHAPTER 13

He paused before opening the door to the cafe, shivering in the midmorning sun. The heavy brass handle, warm and smooth, would need untold energy to transmute into gold, the only proper offering when begging forgiveness.

He shook his head at the impossibility. Twenty pounds of gold would be an insufficient penance for not waking up next to Evangeline. The morning after, every color, every scent, and every sound seemed magnified in vibrancy.

So he took a deep breath, and walked inside.

Evangeline nodded at a customer before freezing in Prospero's gaze. Whether in surprise, shame, or joy, he could not say. All he could manage in response was a sheepish smile.

"Hi."

"Well. Good morning. You, ah, you look nice."

Prospero glanced down. The suit — the one he'd worn to his last alimony hearing—still fit, now a bit loose. Andy had tightened the seams by melding the fabric together, making the suit look tailored, modern, and neat. Prospero showed her how to smooth out the shirt — without a steamer—a feat Andy considered with a severe gaze.

He was about to say something when Angie the manager peeked her head from behind the pastry counter. "Good morning! Is Eve providing everything you need?"

"Yes, thank you," he mumbled. Evangeline smiled at the counter and bit her lip.

"If you need anything else from her—and I mean *anything* else—you just let her know, okay?"

He nodded and wondered why Evangeline pushed her away.

"I'm sorry I left so early. I had to get ready for today."

"Your note was..." she glanced around her, ensuring privacy. "*Graphic.*"

"I just wanted to let you know how I felt. I'm sorry."

"Sorry?" She flashed a wicked stare and glanced to the back of the cafe. "I read it five times. I might lock myself in the bathroom and read it a few more."

He managed a guilty chuckle. "I had a wonderful night."

"Well, I hope that's an understatement."

"I was hoping... I could see you again."

She blossomed into a soft smile. "Didn't you just... leave me?"

"All I wanted was to—" He glanced behind him and leaned close to whisper. "I would've given anything to wake up next to you. But I had to get ready for a meeting. I hate that I had to leave last night."

"You owe me." She said everything with a flick of her hair.

"How can I make it up to you?"

"Will you write me another dirty note?"

"I'll do my best. When's your next break?"

"I'll meet you out back in five minutes."

He nodded as she greeted a pair of snowbirds with a blinding smile.

A few minutes later, Evangeline burst from the back door. She pulled him behind a pile of discarded pallets, hiding them from view.

"Hey, about last night..." What could he say? He tried to find words that conveyed the life-changing experience.

"Evangeline, that was the most beautiful night of my life. I don't know what to say. I've been thinking of you all day." He struggled to string together something that didn't sound ridiculous, when she pulled him by his coat.

"Angie's been teasing me since I walked in this morning."

"Why?"

She raised a knowing eyebrow. "Oh my god, Prospero. Women know."

"You told her? About last night?"

She answered with a delectable smile.

"Should I be embarrassed?"

"More like in demand, but I'm not into sharing." She caressed his cheek, then narrowed her eyes. "What happened to your cut? Did the bandage fall off?"

He froze. "Nothing. I...put some super glue on it. Just in case."

"You don't even have a bruise. But hopefully you'll have a sexy little scar." She raised an eyebrow and melted her lips onto his.

"Why does this feel so right?" she breathed through his lips.

"Maybe... because it is?"

"You are very wise, Mister Jones." She draped her arms around his neck. "So when do I see you again?"

He flushed at the gesture. "Soon. But I have to go to a meeting."

She traced the outline of his coat. "Is that why you're dressed all handsome today?"

He nodded, and she ran her hands further down his coat.

"I could get off for lunch. Make sure you're all nice and relaxed. Give you some inspiration for my next naughty poem."

"I'd love to, but we have to leave soon."

"We? Who's we?"

"This... person who's helping me. It's a long story."

She brought her face inches from his, and hissed. "Is it that woman? The one from yesterday?"

He said nothing before she pulled away and pressed her fists into her head. "Oh god, I'm such an idiot. That's why you left!"

"Evangeline, please..."

She winced and bent over, hiding her face. "Oh god, I should've known..."

"Evangeline, please." He reached for her, but she pulled away. "Andy is a colleague. A cranky, brilliant colleague who's smiled once since I've known her."

"Is she a friend with benefits? Are you sleeping with her? Was that why you left me after we had sex?"

"No!" He shook his head. "I've screwed everything up in my life. But not this. I really don't want to throw away what happened last night."

He caressed her arm, then her hand. This time, she accepted the gesture.

"I'll be back tonight. I promise." He brought her close in an embrace, kissing her forehead, her eyes, and lips before standing back to marvel at her perfection. "I'm going to miss you. Even if it is only for the day."

For a moment she glared back, before her pursed lips melted into a smile. "You'd better. I want another poem."

They kissed again, this time unhurried by the world.

CHAPTER 14

Prospero shielded his eyes from the midday sun. "Remind me again why I needed a suit for this?"

"Because we're meeting someone important." Andy tucked his shirt collar under his coat. "Plus, you're out of practice."

"Out of practice? For what? Looking like a stiff?"

She patted his lapel, then turned and continued down the sidewalk.

Prospero sighed, already sweating under the wool. They'd driven far from Tampa, away from beaches and malls, deep into horse country where flat wetlands gave way to lazy hills. These were towns he'd avoided during his long exile in Florida —too quiet, too still, too much time to think.

Pasco's old town center had seen better centuries. A horse-racing boom had brought the area an avalanche of money that allowed the locals to build up a compact down-town. Years later, a bust in the same industry turned the center into a ghost town. Small businesses had crept back in, opportunistic as mammals after a mass extinction, filling abandoned storefronts on the ground floor. The odd upstairs floor still housed apartments unchanged since the middle of the last century.

Their destination sat above a coffee shop struggling to attract sparse crowds. Behind a large window, in full view of the street, a boy nursed a juice box while his mother scrolled through a visor feed. On the overhead screen, a robotic anchor droned about atrocities in South America, then dissolved into yet another Apex Industries ad. Their familiar CEO beamed with predatory charm.

Andy studied the child and his mother, then glared at the video with barely contained disdain. She turned from the commercial onslaught toward a flight of concrete stairs. Prospero followed, sweat pooling on his back, when Andy knocked on a heavy wooden door, dark with memory. Footsteps shuffled in response from somewhere that sounded airy and bright. The door cracked open, revealing an older man with walnut skin and short white hair. His dark amber eyes filled the space before them.

"Well, hello!" The old man's baritone filled the stairwell as he swept Andy into an embrace. "Andromeda, you've grown more regal since Milan."

"Professor Kinzer," she said with a warm smile. "This is Prospero Jones."

Kinzer narrowed his gaze and nodded. "Is that so? Please. Come in."

Prospero had expected dust and mildew. Instead, Kinzer's flat reminded him of a gallery: walls adorned with paintings, shelves crowded with sculptures, piles of journals bridging gaps between stacks of books. Sunlight poured in through hanging plants, scattering gentle shadows. The air carried a faint aroma of paint and flowers.

"Tea?" Kinzer asked, gesturing toward a small breakfast table. "Chamomile with honey, Andromeda?"

"Thank you," Andy replied, making herself comfortable on a high-backed chair.

Prospero hesitated. "Black, with cream and honey, if it's not too much trouble."

"No trouble at all." Kinzer busied himself with a kettle. Andy tipped her head back, smiling at the soft light streaming from the window.

"Why are we here?" Prospero whispered.

"Ah, that is a question that has baffled us for centuries."

"No, I mean why are we *here*," he said, pressing a finger against the table.

"Because you have some questions," she said. "And he may have some answers."

Kinzer returned with a tray of steaming mugs. "And you have more than questions, Mister Jones."

Prospero bristled. "I'm sorry, Professor, but—"

Kinzer interrupted, holding up a spoon. "No need for apologies. Tell me, does this utensil know it is alive?"

Prospero blinked. "Excuse me?"

"Of course it doesn't. Yet it is made from the same iron that flows in your veins. Here we are—born of the same stars, and yet only we know we exist. Why?"

"Because we have brains?" Prospero replied.

Kinzer smiled. "So does a crow."

He felt trapped. "Because... we're conscious. Or we have a soul."

"Precisely." Kinzer sipped his tea. "Tell me, what do you make of the von Neumann–Wigner interpretation?"

"The what?"

Kinzer's eyes gleamed. "Andromeda has told me about your interests, Mister Jones. No need to act surprised."

He stared slack-jawed at the response. "Is this a test?"

"Not yet, Mister Jones. Not yet."

He pinched his nose and shut his eyes. Any pretense of civility had vanished somewhere between tea and the blunt questions. When he opened them, Kinzer gazed at him with a curious smile. No choice, Prospero thought, but to play along.

"You mean the idea that consciousness affects reality? That reality isn't real until a conscious observer looks at it?"

Kinzer clasped his hands with a wide smile. "Technically, it was about consciousness collapsing the wave function. But yes, that's the one."

Prospero rubbed his temples. "Awareness changes reality."

"Indeed," Kinzer said through a lopsided smile. "And perhaps some minds affect it more than others."

Kinzer produced a coin from his pocket and balanced it on the table's edge. With a knuckle rap, it toppled.

"Quantum decoherence. Ever heard of it?" Prospero was about to reply, but Kinzer was on a roll. "It is what happens when possibilities collapse into outcomes. Like a coin collapsing to either face under the slightest disturbance."

He took a sip of tea, eyes locked on Prospero. "I believe, Mister Jones, that you can somehow prevent decoherence at the level of observed reality."

Kinzer picked up the coin from the table, flipped it, and caught it. "Heads or tails? Change it, Mister Jones."

Prospero tried to swallow away the damn ringing in his ears, an interrupted yawn. Andy shrugged in encouragement. Against his better judgment, he said, "Heads."

Kinzer opened his hand, gleaming with the stern face of a president. Prospero's stomach lurched.

"Again," Kinzer urged. "Tails this time. Don't force it. Just decide it."

He flicked the coin, caught it, and slapped in onto the back of his hand. For a flicker of a moment, Prospero felt something, an impossible vision carried on a wave: both sides of the coin visible, waiting for a nudge.

He nodded. Kinzer opened his hand, and Prospero's stomach fell.

"That proves nothing," Prospero said, his mouth dry. "Luck."

"Then let us banish luck," Kinzer said, retrieving a deck of cards from the bureau. "Andromeda, would you be so kind as to shuffle these?"

She obliged with a silent chuckle. Prospero sat rigid. "You're asking me to pull a rabbit out of a hat."

Kinzer leaned forward. "This is not magic. This is far more than that. A coin is child's play. But this—" He gestured to the deck. "This is the universe."

Cards snapped against each other as Andy shuffled. Prospero tried to ignore the sound.

"Tell me, Mister Jones, what is the probability of shuffling a deck of cards until it is perfectly ordered?"

Prospero let out a low whistle, surprised at the change in topic, but relieved to no longer be the center of attention. "I saw a reel about that once. Almost zero. The number of possible decks is an insane number."

"Insane indeed. If humanity could somehow shuffle billions of decks of cards every millisecond since the beginning of the universe, we still would not scratch the number."

Prospero's head swam with the concept, a pressure at the edge of his awareness.

"And now, Mister Jones, you will defeat that enormity.

Andromeda will continue shuffling until you decide on the order."

Decide the order? Kinzer was asking him to wait until Andy sifted all the sand on every beach on earth trillions of times, until she found one specific speck. The probability was unthinkable.

"Please, Mister Jones. Whenever you choose."

He stared at Andy, and something fluttered at the edge of sight. But "seeing" wasn't the correct description. Whatever perception he sensed was not hiding—it was more an understanding, a sense: knowing where your hand was without opening your eyes, or being aware that sunlight was warmer than shadow. He didn't have to wait until he felt it.

In the end, he simply determined it. "Stop."

Andy dealt. One by one, the cards fell into perfect order. Ace through king, suit by suit. His mind roared as the soft, rhythmic slap of each card broke the silence.

Kinzer whispered, "Do you believe us now?"

He stared as Andy finished dealing. A perfectly ordered set —aces, hearts, clubs, then diamonds—lay before her. For a while, no one spoke.

"You're playing a trick on me," he said, feeling parched.

"No tricks, Mister Jones. You collapsed the probabilities. Quantum decoherence overcome at a macroscopic level. You changed the world."

Prospero tried to swallow. "That's... impossible."

"So is quantum mechanics," Andy countered, calm as ever.

Kinzer's tone sharpened. "Tell me, when you saved that woman from the car—what did you see?"

Prospero flinched. "What did she tell you?"

"Not enough. Why don't you tell me?"

He glanced at Andy for support and found none. "I... knew.

The driver was texting. The woman was thinking about groceries. Someone was about to scream. I saw the scene before it happened."

"Then you changed the outcome," Kinzer said.

"No, I didn't..." His protest faltered. He thought of Luke collapsing in the alley, the roar of voices in his mind as electricity hummed through the ground. He thought of forging bismuth through nothing but thought and felt his chest tighten.

Kinzer's eyes glowed with recognition. "You are entangled, Mister Jones. With every soul before you."

Prospero staggered to the window. Outside, passersby shuffled with heads buried in their visors, blind to the street, blind to one another. No children ran. No laughter rose. The world felt brittle and thin.

"You do know what entanglement is, Mister Jones? Once two particles share information, a change in one affects the other. No matter the distance. Imagine that—but with every soul across history."

Prospero swallowed hard. "This is... preposterous."

"Perhaps. Or perhaps you are not the first. History named them saints, witches, demons. Now we know better, and now one of them stands before me."

Something cold slithered down his back.

"But there is more." Kinzer turned grave. "The many-worlds interpretation tells us each choice spawns universes. Some of us believe they are also entangled. If that is so... one madman, one collapse, could threaten all."

Andy's voice dropped to a whisper. "Terminate one universe, end them all."

Prospero spun. "That's impossible." The word seemed overused this afternoon.

"So is everything we've witnessed today," Kinzer replied.

Andy and Kinzer shared an unspoken nod, clearing the table in silence. As they stepped to the door, Andy hugged the old man while Prospero stood rooted to the floor, trying not to faint. The professor clasped his shoulder with surprising strength.

"Remember this, Mister Jones: consciousness is not separate from the universe. It *is* the universe. When one hundred billion minds sense together, they shape reality itself."

Prospero forced a nod, too overwhelmed for words. Kinzer's amber eyes softened.

"And they may do it through you. Do not forget that."

They descended into the street, the late sun casting long shadows. The boy in the coffee shop still sat at his table, eyes glued to his tablet. His mother was gone. The child's small body sagged forward, oblivious, swallowed by a world within a screen. Above him, another Apex ad promised transcendence through distraction.

Andy paused, gaze lingering. A flicker of pain crossed her face, then hardened into resolve. She touched Prospero's arm. "Let's get you home."

CHAPTER 15

Mullet Cove had changed.

Prospero knew it hadn't—it was still the same town he'd once hated, with the same red brick streets, the same crooked lamp posts lining Main Street—but something *felt* different.

It had been just a day. One impossible day. But *he* had changed.

"All that really happened, then?"

Andy motioned to the driver to wait, and crossed her arms. "It did. I know it is a lot to accept."

He shook his head. "You can say that again."

"Take some time. Spend some time with her. We'll speak soon."

He nodded—even a handshake seemed too much—and waved as Andy and another nameless driver drove away.

He walked past the coffee shop, hoping against hope that Evangeline would still be there. The "closed" sign hung crooked inside the glass pane. Everybody was gone.

For everyone else in this world, reconnecting after a long day would've been simple: call them using your watch, handset, or glasses. But neither he nor Evangeline owned anything more complex than a *Chirp*, the pejorative nickname given to the bare-bones handsets handed to the elderly. Because as the industry knew, even young children needed pocket-sized supercomputers taking every second of their attention.

He wished he could see her when last night's image burst into his mind. A bright tug, a warm spot somewhere in his thoughts: Bobby's, half a block north, still hopping on a slow night.

The dim glow of a neon beer sign flickered off a street sign as he stepped inside. Evangeline glanced up from the bar, strands of hair caressing her cheeks as she smiled.

"I knew you'd find me," she said, sliding a glass of wine toward him. "Got you something."

He slid onto the stool next to her, avoiding the urge to lean in for a kiss.

"You okay?"

He blew his cheeks out. "Yeah. It's been a long day." But right now, things were perfect.

She took a sip, then propped her chin in her hand. "Tell me."

Prospero drummed his fingers on the bar. When he looked in her eyes, the insanity of the past hours vanished, a cloud lost below a horizon.

"Andy drove me all the way to Pasco to meet one of her mentors."

Her eyes narrowed, and her lips pressed tight. She set her glass down and tilted her head. "Oh?"

"It wasn't like that," Prospero replied. "It was more of a— quiz."

She arched an eyebrow. "A *quiz*."

"Yeah," he replied. At the far end of the bar, an older

gentleman played solitaire. Prospero sipped his wine, hoping his hands would not tremble. "Quantum mechanics. Philosophy. The nature of reality. Whether consciousness has a role to play in the natural world." He hoped he wouldn't have to explain the coin or the cards. Instead, she looked away.

"Of course, consciousness changes the world. Duh."

This was not what he had expected. "Really?"

"Of *course*. I can decide to drop this wineglass on the floor." She glanced at Bobby and gestured *I'm kidding*. "That would change reality. Every choice we make changes reality."

"You have a point. I think he was talking more about the quantum world."

"Oh! Von Neumann and Wigner?"

He set the glass down and stared. She delicately pushed his chin to close his mouth.

"Intro to quantum mechanics was a core class at Gainesville. Don't ask me why." She winked and took another sip of wine. "Did I surprise you?"

"You always surprise me. So, what do you think about it?"

She took a deep sigh and laid her chin on her palm. "One day, science and religion will be the same thing. Reality reminds me of a bunch of blind men groping an elephant. Religion says 'it's a snake', or 'it's a tree', while science tries to figure out its mass and volume." She shrugged with a playful grin. "Both miss the fact that it's a cute elephant with long eyelashes."

"I have to say, that is the most unique explanation I've heard in... ever. The man I met, Professor Kinzer, was Wigner's protégé."

"You met Devdan Kinzer?"

The look on his face must've been the reason she laughed.

"He was a visiting professor a few years back. I listened in on a seminar. He was amazing. He's here in state?"

"Pasco," Prospero replied with a nod. "You surprise me more every day, Evangeline."

She stuck out her tongue in playful retort. "Sometimes I wonder what would've happened if I'd forgotten about marine biology and focused on physics or cognitive science. I just saw that a pair of scientists published a thought experiment where the only logical outcome was disproving the assumption that consciousness did not exist."

He swirled the wine in the glass, smiling at the connection. "I hope someday science grows up to understand what some religions say about the mind."

She blew him a kiss in appreciation. "I just hope billionaires like Maxwell Salvatore don't screw everything up before that happens."

Prospero stiffened. "The CEO of Apex? Why him?"

She let out a breathy laugh. "Because I think he wants all of us as slaves. Everything Apex sells captures attention and takes away choice. His phones, those damn glasses, the watches... he collects all this data on everyone so they don't ever have to decide. Every interaction is now curated. I think it's pathetic. I think *he's* pathetic."

"That's why you don't have wireless in the cafe."

"Exactly. So people can talk."

"Come on," he said, pushing back from the bar. "Let's go for a walk."

They strolled through town as the last remnants of sunset turned to night. The conversation drifted between philosophy, the "many worlds" and the Copenhagen interpretations of quantum mechanics, a few off-color jokes, and whether anything scientists had observed actually happened in the material world.

The more they talked, the more he wanted to tell her everything: Kinzer and his questions, the impossible things he'd done with both of them watching. Impossibilities unfolded inside him, and he had no way to tell her.

She'd think he was crazy. And if he showed her, she'd think *she* was crazy.

They turned the corner where Luke had slammed onto the pavement. Nothing remained of the moment he'd almost ended a man's life, using only thought. He shivered and stole a glance at Evangeline, who still laughed at her own joke, unaware of the seething in his mind.

He'd almost killed a man. What would Evangeline do when she found out?

He was still considering that disturbing thought when they arrived at Evangeline's. She stopped at the little staircase leading up to her second-floor door and turned.

"Are you coming in?"

He'd first seen her eighteen months ago. Sometime after that, they shared their first conversation. Over time they'd become friendly, if not friends. Last night, his most impossible dream had come true. And tonight he understood that the bond between them was deeper than he could've imagined.

He could manipulate energy, change probability, and read minds. But this he wouldn't dare screw up.

"I'd love to, but..."

"But... what?"

He took a deep breath to calm his nerves. "I don't want you to think I only like you because you're gorgeous and amazing in bed." He tried to smile but swallowed instead. "I love being with you. I want to be with you every moment of every day. But I don't want you to get tired of me. So if you need to be alone tonight, I understand."

For a long while, she just stared. Then, a smile curled the edges of her perfect lips.

"Well," she said, turning toward the stairs. "That's good to know."

His stomach dropped. He'd become a master at failure by trying to do the right thing.

Evangeline climbed one step and turned back. "Do you remember Valentine's Day last year?"

He froze as shame erupted through his skin.

"I was having a really bad time. I'd stopped working on my dissertation, moved down here to find myself, and had a nasty breakup with a complete asshole. I was going to have the worst Valentine's Day ever. Do you remember?"

His neck burned. "I think so..."

"I walked into the coffee shop and found a bouquet of yellow roses and daisies. With my name on it."

He tried to shrug but grimaced instead.

"Not exactly traditional. Which was perfect. Then I read the note. And cried."

He stared at the ground. "Whoever wrote that must've—"

"I knew you sent them." She stepped down and placed her hands on his chest. "I hadn't told anyone what had happened. There was no one I could trust. But I always felt I could share things with you. You were the only person who listened. And you were so noble, trying to pretend it wasn't you."

She touched his chin and stared into his soul.

"I still have the card. And I dried one flower, saving it so I could remember something so sweet and romantic. You cared, Prospero. You just wanted me to feel better, and you didn't want me to know."

A half-shrug was his last remaining defense.

"So, no, Prospero. I don't want to be alone tonight. I want to talk, and drink wine, and laugh and cry together, and maybe…" She leaned to whisper in his ear. "Inspire my next poem."

She climbed the steps and opened her door. An orange light spilled out, lighting her hair in a fiery halo.

"Are you coming?"

For a moment, he hesitated. The world was fragile, uncertain. Was this the right choice?

Then he broke into a smile, and leapt up the stairs after her.

CHAPTER 16

For the first time in years, Prospero did not wake up to regret. Outside, Mullet Cove stirred without urgency. In here, time stopped.

Sunbeams filtered through the curtains, casting amber streaks on the ceiling. Everything felt impossibly real, as if the universe itself was giving him permission to linger. He turned his head to admire Evangeline—the way her hair fanned out across the pillow, the way her lips parted in sleep, the rise and fall of her breathing.

The apartment smelled like her—something floral, but earthy and warm. He exhaled, feeling the sheets tangled around their legs, the weight of her arm draped over his chest. He savored her scent, her utter perfection, and wished he could somehow match his heartbeat to hers. The only bad thing about Evangeline sleeping next to him was that her aquamarine eyes were closed.

She was, after all, the most perfect being in all of creation.

He used to believe in free will. Then the world broke him. Now, fate had delivered something impossible, just as he discovered the one place where he belonged. Could something this perfect be real? Could he ever deserve this?

This was *real*; and the first choice that had felt right.

He toyed with a lock of her hair, savoring the memory of her gaze during another unforgettable night—when Andy's voice ripped into his mind.

I rescued you because you have to save the world.

The terror in Kinzer's eyes when he said *Do you believe us now?*

Luke. Bismuth.

What the hell was going on? And why was he thinking about any of this, instead of Evangeline's skin on his?

Why did it feel like everything was about to be taken away?

His hand stilled against Evangeline's skin. A golden beam of sunlight played against the curve of her bare shoulder, lighting up strands of her hair. A sudden, irrational fear clenched him—this instant would be gone forever. He'd spent so much of his life running from the past that he could not hold the present.

Evangeline stirred, mumbling something incoherent before pressing her face into the crook of his neck. "Mmm," she murmured. "Stop thinking so loud."

Prospero let out a breath. "What do you mean?"

"I know you." She shifted, pressing a luscious kiss against his jaw. "Your heart's racing like you just escaped a close call."

If she only knew... He exhaled, trying to still his heart. He caressed her arm and her back, and she groaned with delight.

For an instant, he thought about telling her everything. About Andy; about Kinzer. About the impossibilities shifting inside him, the things he had done in the past two days that defied everything he understood about the world.

Instead, he reached for her, tucked a strand of hair behind her ear, and whispered, "You have no idea how much I don't want to leave this bed."

"So don't. You must be so tired…" She pressed her body against his and giggled, sharing the secret of another unforgettable night. He'd have lots to write about in his next poem.

He kissed her hair again, and for a moment, everything seemed perfect.

But something or someone blasted into his mind.

Nothing perfect is meant to last.

He shuddered at the thought, closing his eyes to focus on the moment. The weight of Evangeline's body against his, the warmth of her skin, the delicate scent of her hair… these were here, now. Whatever lay beyond could never take this away.

Could it?

"Are you okay? You just gasped like something startled you."

"Just… thinking."

"Well, I have to go to work today." She slipped her legs over him, and whispered into his ear. "But I don't have to be there just yet."

The world unfolded in vibrant color on the walk back to his apartment. A few days ago he'd felt it: the hyper-reality when he'd sensed the order of the world lying beyond everything surrounding him. Evangeline had the same impact. Her presence, her insight, her smile made the world more real. How unfathomably fortunate that their lives had crossed.

The unforgettable images of the morning played back in his mind. Evangeline catching her breath as amber light caressed her skin. The indescribable color of her eyes as they kissed and said, *see you soon.* Her last desperate embrace, when she pulled him back to make sure he'd remember her.

He opened the door, beaming at the memory, and stopped.

"Hard to keep tabs on you."

Andy sat at his kitchen table, arms and legs crossed, as if she belonged there.

"How'd you get in?"

She stood and smiled. "You already know that. Did you get enough sleep?"

"I—yes, I did."

"You don't have to lie to me. Let's go."

"Go? Where?"

"Someone else you have to meet. Today."

"But I just walked in!" He knew the retort wouldn't matter. Andy operated in a world where everything bent to her will.

"I know," she said, and stared with a curious smile. "Unfortunately, the world doesn't care about our timelines. I'll wait outside while you change."

"But... I—"

"Don't worry. We'll pass by the coffee shop first."

CHAPTER 17

Over years of visits, Prospero had become attuned to the ebb and flow of Sirius Java. On certain days, at certain times, a flood of visitors descended into the quiet space, driving a sprint that somehow vanished in minutes. On this morning the rush had passed, leaving a handful of regulars catching up on gossip, and working on scattered tables. Evangeline, her back towards the entrance, chatted with Angie, the manager, about something of interest. The moment he entered, Angie lit up, her eyes darting between them.

"Well, good morning," Angie sang out, drying her hands on a towel. "You look exhausted! Like you had a *really* long night? Can Eve get you anything else?"

"Angie, please!" Evangeline tried to push her away, but Angie stood her ground with barely contained glee.

"Eve, I'm just trying to help an amazing poet. I wonder what inspired him last night?"

Evangeline turned beet red at the comment. Prospero joined her, staring at the ground. "I liked it better when you ignored me."

"I think that's a lie," Angie replied with a grin, before Evangeline pushed her away.

"I'm so sorry about her."

"She's insistent, I'll say that. Got a few minutes to talk?"

"Sure." She gestured at Angie as they moved to a quiet table under a window. Prospero leaned forward, bracing himself on his elbows. Evangeline surprised him by reaching for his hand.

"I really enjoyed our evening," she whispered. "And our morning."

"I guess I owe you some more verse."

"Two, by my count." She leaned in and drilled her eyes into his. "One should be long and slow, like an epic poem. And the next one should be emphatic, and wild, and loud, and—"

He leaned closer and whispered. "People can hear us!"

"I'm sorry. I was talking poetry." She smiled and winked. "Nothing else."

"I have another meeting this afternoon."

"Is that why you're dressing up now? I've always been a hippie chick, but I'm kind of liking this business side of you. Tell Andy I'm keeping my eye on her."

"She's very impertinent. And pushy."

"Who are you meeting?"

He took a deep breath. "I'm meeting Maxwell Salvatore."

The warmth in her eyes vanished. "No."

"Evangeline—"

"The CEO of Apex? You can't be serious." She stared as if waiting for him to take it back. When he didn't, she stood up, shoved her chair back, and stormed out the back door.

He found her pacing around the pallets in the loading area. "What the heck, Prospero? Why didn't you tell me?" She pulled her hair back.

"Tell you what? It's just a meeting."

She pointed toward the street. "It's never 'just a meeting' with assholes like that. That transactional bastard is the reason the world is crumbling. The guy who's buying all these social media companies now controls what everyone sees, and hears, and thinks. He's a fucking trillionaire without a soul. What are you doing with him? What is that woman doing to you?"

"It's... complicated."

"Complicated?" She let out a bitter laugh. "You know what's not complicated? The fact that people like him want to own the world. And the worst part? Everyone just lets them."

"Something important is happening, Evangeline. I don't understand it myself. But as soon as I come back, I'll let you know."

"What the hell is he doing here? Is Andy helping him buy the city like he did with Fremont?"

"Apparently, he has an office downtown, now that he's building that warehouse up the road. We managed to schedule a meeting with him."

"A meeting? For what?"

Prospero stood in awe of the fire in her eyes, the certainty in her voice. Once, he'd wanted to tell her every-thing. Now, sitting here, he wasn't sure of anything, including himself.

"I just have to do this."

Evangeline stared. "You just have to talk to the richest man in the world, the person who is stealing everyone's atten-tion and opinion and judgment, who is numbing every damn person who buys any of his poison, because your new friend told you, and you don't know why?"

"It's not exactly like that..."

She turned to the door. "I hope you know what you're doing."

"Evangeline, please."

He reached into his pocket and placed the pebble in her hand.

"What's this?"

"It's bismuth."

She turned the stone over in her fingers, examining it with a confused scowl. "What am I supposed to do with this?"

"Keep it," Prospero said. "It's not from around here. I'll come back for it."

She stared back, lips curled in a disappointed sneer. "You'd better."

Then she turned and walked inside, slamming the door behind her.

CHAPTER 18

They stepped out of the car into the cooling afternoon without a word to their driver, watching the world reflected on tall glass windows facing the busy street.

"You sure know how to pick them." Prospero gazed straight up at the sheer walls of a glass high-rise towering over the Hillsborough River. Flashes from an orange sunset glinted off sheer expanses of polished metal and stone. He'd somehow overlooked this structure every time he'd visited the Riverwalk.

"He's up there?"

"Penthouse office. They're expecting you at the front desk."

He nodded and stepped towards the door, and noticed Andy standing her ground on the sidewalk. "You coming?"

"This is where I leave you," she said. "You'll be meeting Maxwell Salvatore alone."

Prospero blinked in surprise. "What do you mean, alone? You came all this way to drop me off?"

Andy nodded. "This meeting is for you. Only you."

"You're telling me now? I don't mean to be a clue bag, but what the hell am I supposed to say to him?"

"You'll know. I'll meet you when you're done."

"Here?" He waved an open palm around Ashley Drive. "How am I going to find you?"

She tapped her finger on her forehead and walked off.

All of this felt like too much. He'd walked from the back alley of the coffee shop after Evangeline walked away, only to find Andy waiting for him outside the alley. No explanation nor mention of how she'd found him. They entered a black sedan—Prospero thought it was a ride share—and drove against end-of-work traffic all the way to downtown Tampa.

Halfway through the causeway, Prospero noticed. Andy hadn't once looked at their driver or pulled out a phone. They didn't even speak. The silence allowed him plenty of time to remember Evangeline's anger at the upcoming meeting. Instead of enjoying the late afternoon, the cool bay breeze, or delighting in the soft sting of sand, couples walking the bike path stared at invisible worlds, their chins jutting out in utter rejection of each other. Without looking, Prospero knew what company had manufactured the devices that sucked the couple's attention and will. In minutes, he'd meet the CEO.

That's when his palms began to sweat. Panic overtook him: would Evangeline still be there when he returned? After this morning's parting, why would she ever choose him? He glanced at Andy, perhaps searching for support. She stared out her own window, severe and reserved, perhaps judging him in silence.

The gentle lurch of the elevator snapped him out of the memory. Despite the long drive, Andy provided no information about the visit. Prospero hadn't worried, assuming she'd be leading the conversation. When Prospero asked—somewhat sarcastically—what topic they would discuss, Andy demurred.

"You'll find out," she said, giving no further explanation for meeting a trillionaire, for the crazy magic tricks he could now perform, for her ability to pop into and out of his life with neither warning nor trace. Days ago he thought Andy was a con woman or a secret agent. Meeting Kinzer—someone known to Evangeline, but not him—had shaken something different inside him. Now, as he jetted up a sleek elevator to meet the most powerful man in the world, he reexamined the experience and wondered if this was still a con job—and how she'd pulled it off.

But unless he was about to stop at the next floor and return to the lobby, he had no choice but to trust her—despite a hollow gnawing that this was a cosmic joke.

He cleared his ears from the change in pressure on the trip up. The doors opened onto the penthouse floor, and Prospero gasped. Floor-to-ceiling windows wrapped the entire space, providing an astonishing view of the Tampa cityscape. At this height, the sunset—far beyond the exurbs, the beaches, the Gulf itself—dominated the horizon, an omnipotent deity scoffing at the serfs in a vast kingdom. He stepped into a carpeted lobby, admiring the sleek decor and stylish furniture. This was luxury beyond anything he could comprehend.

The receptionist, a stunning young woman with a jet-black pixie cut and dead eyes, stood from behind a polished granite desk. She hid behind trendy glasses Prospero recognized as the latest digital accessory.

"Hello Mister Jones. My name is Arabella. Mr. Salvatore is expecting you."

There was no warmth or agency in her voice. The young woman knew who he was. He followed her gesture towards a set of double doors, and into a conference room oozing with intimidation.

Salvatore, CEO of the most valuable company on the planet, sat at the end of a massive table, leaning back in an expensive-looking leather chair. He looked younger than Prospero expected, less artificial than in the many Apex ads he'd shot. The handsome features of someone accustomed to getting his way chiseled his face, and his eyes belied secrets or an old soul. Maxwell Salvatore seemed the type of man who sought comfort in bending others to his will.

"Prospero Jones." A smile curled one edges of his lips. "You have no idea why you're here, do you?"

He stopped. "I, uh, hello. I'm afraid I don't."

"Please tell me she didn't tell you anything about saving the world."

Prospero's stomach fell. "She... who?"

Maxwell Salvatore raised a hand to silence him. The movement struck Prospero as ancient: less a gesture of impatience, or a signal of domination.

"I heard you've been talking to Andromeda Vestal, my ex-wife?"

CHAPTER 19

Silence roared in Prospero's ears.

"You know Andy Vestal? She was your *wife?*"

"I've known her for an age. Married about that long."

Prospero caught a sharp breath. "I... uh..."

"It is quite fine, Mister Jones." He walked around the vast, empty desk and offered a warm handshake. "What did she tell you?"

"She, uh..." The orange rays of a stunning sunset bathed the office in soft light. Prospero wished for nothing more than to sit on the sand, watching the clouds with Evangeline; anywhere but here, confessing to the most powerful man in the world that his ex-wife was a con artist. "She set up a meeting, dropped me off, and said I should meet you alone."

"Is that so?" Salvatore unleashed something unexpected: a smile.

"That's all, I swear. I'm as lost as you are."

Salvatore stared at the floor and stuffed his hands in his pockets. This smile was not the grimace he wielded during interviews on business shows. "Did she give you the speech about the forces of nature? Showed you a couple of tricks?" He wrinkled his nose at the secret, a fellow victim. "Told you something about saving the world?"

His throat turned thick, and his neck tingled. Once again, Prospero had failed to learn his lesson. He'd trusted the wrong person—again.

"Waving her hands," Salvatore continued, "and sharing impossible dreams. Talking about insane concepts explainable by science." He gestured air quotes at the last one, as if poking fun at himself. This man—friendly and familiar—was a far cry from the omnipotent trillionaire Prospero had met moments ago.

"It was a farce, Mister Jones. All of it. I'm sorry my ex-wife tried to mislead you. None of her imagined crusades are real." Salvatore stepped close and flashed a sheepish grin. "Never trust a beautiful woman. Even one past her prime."

Maxwell Salvatore glanced out the door and nodded to his assistant.

Prospero swallowed, although he didn't need to, and felt his heart flutter in his neck. The last vestiges of day lit up the edges of faraway buildings in soft pink, as city lights began dominating the night. Somewhere out there, someone enjoyed that perfect time of day, when workplaces empty and hurry yields to night. He ached to share that moment with Evangeline and beg for her forgiveness. He'd fallen for a ridiculous meeting with the most powerful man on the planet instead of staying with her at Mullet Cove, inspiring her next poem.

"I'm so sorry, Mister Salvatore. I didn't mean to waste your time."

"That's quite fine, Mister Jones. We now have something

in common." They stood shoulder to shoulder, admiring the view. "Tell me, what kind of work do you do?"

The urge to lie almost overpowered him. "Engineer by education. Short stint in the military." He stared at his feet, then gazed out at the horizon. "Married the high-school sweetheart who expected more. Lost a daughter at birth. Everything crumbled from there."

Salvatore stiffened. "I thank you for your service. And my deepest sympathies for your loss. We are always escaping so much misery in the world." He paused for a moment, staring deep into Prospero's eyes. "We never quite recover from the loss of a loved one. No matter when or where it happens."

He thought of Evangeline, and almost replied that the world also held great hope—and now that he'd seen it, unfathomable beauty.

"My ex-wife also has a knack for putting me in uncomfortable situations," Prospero replied instead. "I didn't expect us to have that in common."

Salvatore tilted his head back in a quiet chuckle. "Andromeda has stooped to crass tricks. Perhaps she is in her twilight. Diminished by age, or failing health."

"Is she sick?"

"We all become so in time. In greater or lesser degrees."

He nodded in assent. Salvatore, in only a few minutes, had shown more humanity than many of the people he knew.

His reflection caught his eye: surprise, almost relief at having navigated an epic embarrassment. Despite the hate at himself, he ached to share the story with Evangeline. Many would give anything to meet the richest man in the world. Those same people would've died of embarrassment tonight. Only Evangeline would understand his desperation to leave.

"Well, she may have her faults, but she was decent to me.

She even showed me..." Prospero stopped himself. "She shared her friendship. Again, I'm sorry I bothered you. I'll be on my way."

Salvatore tilted his head. "What did she share?"

"Nothing personal. Just... science stuff. Meditation."

"Did she share those with you?" Salvatore leaned in for a whisper. "Or did she show you?"

He swallowed hard: the world's most powerful man suspected he was doing something inappropriate with his ex-wife.

"It wasn't anything like that, Mister Salvatore. She showed me kindness. Nothing more."

He offered his hand, an admission of defeat. Maxwell Salvatore took it, and held on.

"What *did* she show you, Mister Jones?"

Salvatore squeezed until Prospero imagined his bones would crack. He tried to pull back, but Maxwell held firm.

"Did she teach you something like... this?"

Salvatore's grip tightened, and every chair slammed back with a metallic grate.

"Or this?" The skyline shimmered, and a pane of glass turned to sand, spilling an ocean wind into the room.

"Or perhaps, this?"

His insides screamed, a pain greater than anything he'd imagined. Maxwell released his hand, and Prospero collapsed onto the carpet, struggling for breath.

"What...what did you do?"

"I'm afraid Andromeda has shown you something terrible, Prospero Jones."

He looked up through ragged gulps. "What is going on?"

"Tell me, Prospero. What can *you* do?"

His mind roared. *Get out. Get out!*

Wind burst into the room, blasting them with sand, pulling Prospero out. Salvatore raised a hand, and the gale stopped. The open window pulsed as an invisible barrier buffeted against the blast. Prospero gulped air as his limbs shook from the damage.

Salvatore stood and clasped his hands, flashing a wide grin. "Well, it seems you do know a few things, Prospero Jones. Andromeda has always been so impatient."

"What do you mean?" He gasped for words through the throbbing in his chest.

"Did she take you to meet old Devdan? That hippie freak?"

Whatever he'd tried to do had abated. An errant gust blew sand over him, then all was still. "You know Kinzer?"

"Of course, Prospero. A brilliant and misguided old fool." He opened his fist, and Prospero's ribs followed suit.

"Humanity is on the wrong path," he heard through his screams. "A banal existence leading to ruin. I will save them."

Then nothing, as if Maxwell Salvatore turned off the torture only to hear him speak.

The door to the penthouse lobby was still open. He tried to mouth something, anything to gain the attention of the girl at the desk. She stared back, eyes blank, then turned away. She looked just like Andy.

"Save them from what? What are you talking about?"

"I will save them from themselves, of course." He grabbed Prospero's chin and stared into his soul. "Why do you think I've come to this hellhole? Why have I built so much, so soon, to give the world what they think they need? Salvation has already started."

He pushed down the pain and looked up at his tormentor. "Started?"

"Yes, Prospero. It seems much of the world thirsts to be rid of decisions. I'll provide that fate for them."

"You're crazy..."

"No, Prospero. I'm rich, intelligent enough to change the course of history, and I will save us all. I will start here."

"That's... you're insane..."

"Andromeda was never the best judge of character. Or ability. She sent you here to *stop* me? Look at you."

He lifted him up by the neck, hands implacable as steel. Prospero held on, desperate for air, and Maxwell Salvatore dangled him out the window that moments earlier had turned to sand. Vicious wind whipped up from the nothingness yawning below him. He grabbed Salvatore's wrist.

"Who *are* you?"

"One who learned the truth."

"What truth?"

"Andromeda was right about one thing, Mister Jones. Consciousness never dies. Your mind will be one more drop in an ocean I will save. All pain will soon be over, and your souls will remain forever unencumbered by free will. But you will not suffer, and your souls will never extinguish."

He unfurled a sad smile. "And we will all survive, Prospero Jones. I will save them. I will save us all."

"Save us? From what?"

"From ourselves, of course."

He held Prospero over the void. Wind tore at him; the glass skyscraper plummeted toward the yawning ground below. In that split-second, he saw her—Evangeline's eyes, her hair in the breeze, caressing her skin—and ached for every moment not spent with her. He'd never see her again.

"Goodbye, Prospero Jones. Death and life are petals from

the same flower. You and Evangeline will bloom in my garden when I save you from your fate."

Then Maxwell Salvatore let go, and Prospero roared to his death, hundreds of feet below.

CHAPTER 20

Speed.

Water.

Wind.

The street raced to meet him, faster than fear.

Change the outcome.

Wind—relentless and loud—roared in a new direction, now behind him, pushing him past the Riverwalk, onto the surface of the river.

He skipped once, twice, three times, cartwheeling with brutal ferocity, before slapping onto the brackish water, which swallowed him in a lazy wave.

Then nothing. Prospero hung, feet below the surface, again. The lights of the Tampa skyline danced in blurs above him.

It took a moment to realize he was alive. How? He'd fallen from the top of a skyscraper and landed in a river. Impossible, except...

He clenched his mouth, hoping not to drown, and noticed

lights above him. After a couple of strokes, he broke the surface. Air had never tasted so sweet.

"Jeez, he's alive! Dude, are you okay?"

A river taxi carrying a handful of now-excited tourists pulled alongside him. Someone threw a life preserver, landing an arm's length away with a wet splat. He grabbed it, still in his suit.

"He's alive! Holy shit, he's alive! Call emergency!"

"No. Please. Don't call."

"Dude, we have to report this—"

"No. Please. My ex-wife can't find out."

A wide man with a bushy mustache and tight polo waved his finger then ran it across his neck in a clear "knock it off" signal. They pulled Prospero in through a rickety gate at the boat's stern, and he collapsed onto the wet metal deck. Everything hurt.

"You okay?"

He nodded, inventorying his injuries. The squishy, wet suit would freeze him soon, even in the humidity of a Tampa night. He needed a change of clothes or a stiff drink. Preferably both.

"Geez, man, what the hell was that? You were cartwheeling across the river!"

He gulped in air before answering. "Trying to do some tricks on one of those scooters. Flew into the water." Prospero had no idea how he'd arrived at that improbable excuse. Right now it sounded magnificent, and profoundly improbable.

Because he'd fallen from a skyscraper, and lived.

Had he cratered onto the pavement, his remains would've been indistinguishable from gravy. Hitting water at the same force should've liquefied his bones and exploded his abdomen into an unseemly mess.

But somehow, he was alive. He considered how on earth that could've happened, when Kinzer's words rang in his mind.

Just decide the outcome.

"Hey man, I think you're better off just chilling here until—"

"I'm fine. I swear." He was, in fact, fine. Unnaturally, impossibly, paradoxically fine. Other than being drenched to the bone, and feeling like a worn punching bag after having fallen five hundred feet. Prospero Jones was alive. He flexed his joints and took a deep breath. Nothing broken, dislocated, or exploded. Unbelievable.

Just Decide.

"You got a bathroom?"

The man with the bushy mustache—his brass-colored name tag read "Captain"—gestured with his head. "Near the bow. Need a towel?"

"I'm good. Thanks."

He squished his way into the small water taxi's cabin, past a handful of bewildered tourists all wearing a variety of sports paraphernalia, watching him through a panoply of AR glasses. He shut the door behind him, and soon warmed up in the cramped space that smelled of urine, vomit, and something blue. The wet, tired face staring back from the mirror seethed with the impossible.

Salvatore knew. He'd been married to Andy, and understood whatever the hell she'd taught him.

Then he'd tried to kill him.

And if all of that wasn't insane enough... he was alive. A violent gust of wind skidded him across the Hillsborough River, missing the bridge by feet. He'd yard-saled onto moving water, cartwheeling to a stop before slamming onto the shore.

He should be dead.

Instead, he was freezing, and about to suffer a serious bout of hypothermia.

The suit, he remembered with an ember of pride, was a wool blend. After only a few minutes, the fabric had already shed a surprising amount of water. But his shirt and socks and underwear would never dry on their own, and he risked freezing in the cool spring air.

He flicked on the fan switch, and a recalcitrant metal grating gave way to an anemic spin. He focused on the sound of the engine somewhere beneath him, turning hydrocarbon bonds into heat and motion. Then he focused on his sleeve, and thought of water evanescing into mist.

It worked. Prospero felt the heat flow, an unseen river wending from combustion through metal into cloth. In moments, the water evanesced into a fog. For a moment he worried about scalding himself as the water boiled off the suit. He didn't have to; the engine's rumble slowed as the energy funneled into water, evaporating it through focus.

Soon his clothes dried enough for his body heat to warm them. He paid extra attention to his shoes, ensuring he didn't sublimate too much and turn them into desiccated hunks of leather. A few minutes later he emerged in a cloud of mist, his suit dry and warm. The boat captain stared in amazement.

"What the hell was that?"

"Wicking fabrics," Prospero replied with a half-smile. "Latest in men's fashion."

The captain shrugged. "I should call the police."

"I just need to find my scooter. Please. My ex-wife is going to kill me."

"How 'bout I drop you off at the park?"

Prospero nodded in thanks. Passengers gawked as he

walked past, before turning back to whatever online fantasy absorbed them.

The boat bumped to a stop at an aluminum dock jutting into the river. Prospero waited as passengers disembarked, their attentions distracted for as long as a judgmental whisper, before returning to the numbing silence of whatever AR stupidity squeezed their minds. He thanked the captain, old enough not to immerse himself in the distraction, then set off north on the Riverwalk, in search of a stiff drink.

He did not notice the figure behind him, falling in step across the shadow of dusk.

CHAPTER 21

The northern reaches of the city glowed a mile distant. Despite the early hours, Prospero struggled to stay awake. Falling from a skyscraper into a river would to that to you, he thought. He followed streets weaving away from the River-walk, crossing into the forgotten parts of Tampa. Still unsure of his destination, he needed to sit, rest, and think.

The night hummed with something hollow. Vehicles and noise and traffic assaulted his ears, but voices were curiously absent from the din. People hunched into their handsets or walked in a daze, filtering the world through a wide variety of handsets and AR devices. Prospero couldn't blame them. The world was a grimy, brutal place, full of pain and disappointment. A few days ago he'd understood how someone might choose to relinquish attention, and hide from the horror.

"I will save them from free will," he murmured from memory, and caught his breath. One man had developed every distraction from the world.

Maxwell Salvatore, the richest man on the planet—and the man who had just tried to kill him.

Who, beyond all reason, shared his same gift. Or curse.

Maxwell Salvatore, tech genius, wizard, or magician; married to either a con woman, a witch, or something more. He'd wielded the forces of nature at a level unimaginable to Prospero moments ago.

Wielding the forces of nature. Two days ago, that phrase would've belonged at an asylum, or a novel.

He stopped at a corner crosswalk as the world wheeled around him. He could hide in plain sight, feet from those whose minds had been numbed by filtering the world. Five years ago, none of this existed. Now, addiction counselors reported that "digital detox" was the number one source of income for an entire industry, and Maxwell Salvatore had been the architect of that change.

Maxwell, the charismatic CEO of Apex Industries, seemed intent on ensuring humanity remained hooked on anything that eschewed the burden of decisions. He'd created an unending torrent of tailored distortion and distraction to destroy the thin veneer between fiction and truth. Prospero, not a prisoner in a manufactured world, wondered if the slow eradication of fact and truth from human minds was precursor or outcome in Maxwell's plan. He knew many who laughed at his unease and alarm at the slow erosion of reality. Many considered him and Evangeline strange for worrying about the dissolution of independent thought.

All while Maxwell Salvatore told over half of the planet what to think, and what to see.

I will save them from free will.

Salvatore's penthouse office—the one where Prospero had almost plummeted to his death minutes ago—loomed distant in the early dark. Could Maxwell see him, even now? He wanted to leave, to be as far as possible from someone so powerful and implacable. Someone who shared—and mastered—a shared secret.

And most importantly, someone who'd tried to kill him.

But where would he escape if given the chance? Somewhere without Evangeline?

Maybe if they were together, he'd be able to share the truth. He shuddered at the thought: he'd been with her only days, and he was already keeping secrets.

A few blocks later, away from the bustle of the Riverwalk, the tall building slipped out of view. He passed an old bar nestled between a real estate office and a chain sub shop, where a faded wooden anchor watched over a worn entrance. He doubled back, taking a spot at a corner of the bar. His sleeves — now bone dry — stuck to the varnished wood. Curved silver taps and glinting liquor bottles beckoned tired souls. But the noise of conversation was absent. Many of the couples looked past each other, engrossed in glasses, or hunched over glowing screens. He'd been so tired of this world that he hadn't noticed it crumbling around him.

"What can I get you?" The bartender looked up from his phone, momentarily distracted from his digital escape.

"Tennessee Crown?" The choice seemed appropriate after the past few days. Beer and booze had long dulled the edges of his disgust as he'd spiraled toward his end. He hadn't expected to drink again, because he had expected to be dead.

Then he remembered six, or seven, or eight glasses of wine with Evangeline, then several more...

He winced at the memory of her. The way her eyes could tell stories with the most delicate glance, the way her parted lips ignited his soul, the delightful thrill when she ventured into some unexpected topic and they lost themselves in conversation.

A few days ago, he'd tried to kill himself. Now he ached to have tomorrow back.

The bartender placed the glass on a coaster, and Prospero took a long swig. The beer—cold, served in elegant tulip glasses because of the kick—soothed every atom of his soul.

I will save us all, Maxwell Salvatore had said an instant before he dropped Prospero to his death. He struggled to remember more of the conversation, to find a truth just out of reach. But fatigue numbed him. He preferred to think of Evangeline, sheets caressing her skin, the sparkle in her eyes as they kissed, the fire when she turned away in disgust at the news of this meeting.

She was right about Maxwell, and maybe right about everything.

"Prospero Jones?"

The voice, sharp and angry, belonged to a young black man with plain glasses, no hair, and a short temper. He dressed far too nicely for this joint: dark suit, white shirt, black tie.

"Who's looking?"

The man slid onto the stool next to his, facing the door, and nodded at the bartender. "Club soda with lemon, please."

"Are you a cop?"

The man shook his head and pulled out a thin black wallet. "Not exactly. Miles Dalton. Department of Justice."

Prospero took a swig of beer. "Am I in trouble, Mister Dalton?"

"Mind answering a few questions?"

"Ask away." Prospero downed his beer and, despite the G-man, signaled the bartender for another. He savored the looming numbness. One more beer and he'd be far from the horror of the past hours, begging forgiveness in Evangeline's arms.

"Did you just meet with Maxwell Salvatore?"

He sat up with a start. "How'd you know that?"

"He's the richest man in the country."

"Probably the richest dude on earth. Is he doing something illegal?"

"You tell me." Dalton sliced him with an accent from up north. "What did you talk about?"

"Not much. Ex-wives, mostly."

Dalton nodded *thanks* to the bartender and regarded Prospero over a sip of soda. "You scheduled a one-on-one meeting with Mister Salvatore? And you talked about your ex-wives?"

Prospero nodded. "Surprised me as well. Guess we all have our pasts."

"Well, that's pretty interesting. May I ask if you talked business?"

"You may. We didn't. I have no business with him."

Dalton took another sip. "Let me get this straight. You manage a meeting with Maxwell Salvatore, the richest man in the country, maybe the world. You talk about your ex-wives, and nothing else."

He wanted to respond with something unkind about Andy manipulating him, but demurred. "That's right."

"Then someone tries to kill him."

"Someone what?"

"You tell me. We have eyewitness reports of a shattered window. While you were in his office."

Prospero stiffened. "Yeah, apparently the window broke."

"And what did you do when the window broke?"

The beer no longer tasted good. "I, uh, took the elevator down."

"That's very interesting." He took a long swig of club soda. "Because none of the cameras saw you take the elevator down. His assistant says you jumped."

The beer's haze was no longer welcome. "Jumped?"

"Into the Hillsborough River. We've got video." He turned his phone, showing Prospero being pulled from the water, suit dripping. Swipe. Another clip—Prospero stepping out of the river taxi's bathroom, dry and composed. "We couldn't recover the parachute."

"The what?"

"The parachute you used to jump out of Maxwell Salvatore's penthouse and onto the bridge."

His mind reeled. How the hell could he explain?

"You were picked up by a water taxi. As if nothing had happened. Almost as if you'd been trained at this, Mister Jones."

"I was fortunate. The wind. It blew me to—"

"Let me help you. I think you tried to kill the richest man in the world, and when it failed, you jumped out and tried to escape. You landed in the river, hid your parachute, and concocted a fantastic story. How am I doing?"

Prospero froze. How could he explain the past hour? "Why would I want to hurt Maxwell Salvatore?"

Dalton stared. "A lot of people want Maxwell Salvatore dead."

"I'm not one of them." He turned back to his beer and noticed his hands shaking.

"We're not sure about that. We have the bar surrounded, Mister Jones. Now, I'm going to ask you to come with me. Please don't make it difficult."

"What? What are you charging me with?"

"Attempted homicide against a public figure. If there's more, please tell me."

It happened fast. Miles Dalton slapped a handcuff — hard, heavy, and cold — onto his wrist, and ratcheted it shut.

"You are under arrest, Mister Jones. You have the right to remain silent..."

The rest of his rights passed in a din. The bartender stood back, surprised but not shocked. Perhaps he considered barstool arrests a normal event. Prospero did not.

Miles swung his hands and cuffed Prospero behind his back.

"I haven't paid."

"On the house," the bartender said, nodding at Dalton.

The rest of the patrons looked up with empty eyes before returning to their screens. One man's gaze lingered—just long enough to see, then not care—as Miles Dalton marched Prospero through the glass door and into a waiting wall of agents.

CHAPTER 22

This cannot be happening.

A black limo loomed ahead, its door a maw he'd never escape. Why he knew this, on a day where everything impossible had happened, Prospero did not know. But the image of him entering the limo seemed a point from which he would never return, an instant that would define his future.

"Mister Dalton, please. I'll talk."

"Are you waiving your right to legal representation?"

Anywhere else, the question would've been met with a harsh "no." But Prospero struggled against something far greater. In just a few days, he'd lifted the veil of everyday life. Competent legal support seemed a low priority. At the moment, staying out of prison seemed the most pressing matter.

"I do. I'll talk. But please. I can't go in there."

Dalton nodded to his friends. "We can hear you better in there."

"No, please! Listen to me." He stood his ground, squeezing his eyes shut to focus. "A woman named Andromeda Vestal set me up for this meeting. I don't know why. She left me in the lobby to meet with Salvatore alone."

Dalton stopped by a female agent with dark, spiky hair. "Okay, buddy, we'll have to—"

"He knew me! Like he had been expecting me. Talking about saving the world or something crazy."

The female agent stiffened at this, but Miles Dalton only pushed Prospero along. "Okay, now we really have to go in the car."

"No! Please let me talk. He knew. He broke the window. Threw me out. Wonder why you haven't recovered a parachute? That man shoved me to my death."

Dalton let out an exasperated breath. "I did a stint in the military as well. No wind is going to push you hundreds of feet across a hundred-foot fall. And I've seen what happens to people who fall from that height. You'd be a puddle on the pavement. Let's go." He grabbed his arm and led him toward the car.

"Mister Dalton, please! Why don't you believe me?"

He sighed like an old man, tired of listening to bullshit. "Because we had an eyewitness. His daughter."

He froze. That bastard had not only lied, he'd framed him. And his assistant Arabella, if that was her real name, was on it. "You might want to check if that really is his daughter."

"Nice try. In you go."

This was it. One day ago, Prospero had stunned a man, turned limestone to marble and then something else. But the back of the car filled him with inexplicable dread.

Maybe because if he went in, he'd never see Evangeline again.

Dalton opened the door and pushed him inside. Prospero stalled, bracing himself against the frame of the door. He felt the rumble of the car's engine and pulled with all his might. The metal on his wrists flaked like rust, warm and dry.

He spread his hands, and the handcuffs—steel turned to brittle antimony—burst open with a soft pop.

Dalton drew his handgun, stepped back, and aimed. "Get down! Hands up and kneel on the ground!"

Prospero knelt, hands above his head. The sidewalk would hold enough heat for what came next.

"Get your hands up!" The female agent yelled from across the hood of the car.

"I just need to steady myself, please." He grunted and placed his palms on the sidewalk.

Waves of heat rose in him, cooling the sidewalk with loud cracks. He glanced at Dalton and the man behind him, focused the roar of energy, then let go. They froze, their weapons still aimed at him.

Suddenly, this was not a good idea.

Time stopped long enough for him to understand. The two armed men struggled to stay upright and conscious, as if they'd suffered a seizure. Their frazzled nerves would clench every muscle, including their trigger fingers. No time to turn the bullets into anything — even talcum at that speed would rip him apart.

So he curled into a ball, turned his clothes impassable, and felt the thunder of hammer blows on his back, hoping for the best.

CHAPTER 23

"Hold Fire! Hold fire! Suspect down, I repeat, suspect is down!"

He registered the screams first. Far away, sirens. Cops or ambulance, he could not tell.

The driver, a young woman with spiky hair and honey eyes, turned him onto his back.

"Fuck. What was that?"

She stood up and aimed at him. "Suspect is alive," she yelled into her lapel. "Suspect is alive, and two agents are down. I need immediate assistance!"

He rubbed his chest, expecting the blood of an exit would. Nothing except the fabric melting back to normalcy, softening back into cotton.

It worked. He took a deep breath, feeling like someone had used his kidneys as a punching bag. The agents had good aim, even when they were falling on their faces. He felt the fabric of the jacket's back turn back to wool, recovering from whatever he'd made. Whatever it was, it had stopped two bullets and left him with the world's most impressive double bruise.

That's when he noticed the red dot on his shirt and realized the female agent was screaming at him.

"I said lie down!" The dot jumped with her screams. "Face down on the ground, now!" Prospero complied, flattening himself on a frosty section of sidewalk.

"Two agents down, I repeat, two agents down. Special Agent Nora Brooks requesting immediate assistance. I repeat, immediate assistance."

The red dot danced on his temple, blazing in his eyes with laser light. He knew—as easily as he could recognize the song of a bird, the sound of a car horn, the laugh of a friend—that the firearm's slide was steel.

He couldn't risk another shot. Plus, the girl seemed the nicest of the three. But transmuting something that far from iron on the periodic table would take a lot of energy.

Good thing he was lying on megatons of dormant heat from the sun. He placed both palms on the sidewalk, still cool from the last feat, and pulled with all his might.

"What the—"

Nora Brooks yelped and dropped her gun. The grip, thermoplastic composite, fell on the sidewalk with a hollow crack. The slide lopped off like an errant ice cream treat on a summer day. A spring, probably titanium, popped free from its prison, a jack-in-the box escaping the metal slurry.

"Stay down!"

Prospero ignored the command. He knelt to see the agent holding a small brick aimed at him. He'd seen enough reels to recognize it: twin electrified leads, designed to bring down a bull. The kids had everything these days.

The staccato whoop of sirens ripped through the roaring in his ears as he realized Miss Congeniality was not going down without a fight. He didn't want to hurt her, but he couldn't stay and chat.

"I'm sorry, miss. I have to go."

He pulled once more. The sidewalk popped and buckled with frost, and the taser cracked open in a cloud of electric fuzz. Agent Nora Brooks dropped it and stepped back with a grimace of horror and understanding.

"You stay down. Please."

"I have to go."

Then she leapt at him—so he pushed back.

Agent Brooks slammed into the back part of the limo with a sickening thud, audible even through the dull peal in his skull. The armor plate yielded little. Nora crumpled to the ground, out cold. Electromagnetism, he remembered from high school, was the force that kept you from sliding into the center of the earth. Very good at repelling matter from itself, or bending motion to your will.

How he could bend it he did not quite know. The question seemed about as useful as asking how Prospero could recognize his own voice, or describing the steps to have a specific thought.

Right now, none of that mattered, so he stood and caught his breath. In the middle of a frosted Tampa sidewalk, three federal law enforcement agents lay unconscious around him. Not a good look while an ocean of sirens closed on him, choking him with sound.

So he ran—away from the sirens, not sure where. He didn't hear them as much as felt them—the noise of engines and surge of electricity and energy. They'd be here in seconds. By then he'd be long gone.

His ribs shrieked in pain from the rounds that slammed into him. He turned the first corner, running against traffic, worried someone might figure out what had happened. He took a hard left, bounding across cars, sliding over hoods, surprised the vehicles moved so slow. Ahead, a door to a parking garage at the base of a hotel or corporate building. He needed somewhere to hide, because he could not outrun this.

He ducked into the unpainted concrete ramp of a parking garage and caught his breath. Andy Vestal, her silhouette lit from the light streaming from an open metal door, gestured wildly and screamed.

"This way!"

He sprinted to the door and slipped into a gray room smelling of solvent.

"Where the fuck have you been?"

That could've been Andy's line. Instead, it was Prospero yelling at the top of his lungs.

"Too much to explain," she said, shutting the door behind him.

They stood in what appeared to be a mix between a storage and a maintenance closet. Metal shelves held cleaning supplies and reams of paper, while an odd assortment of pipes painted blue and red dominated a corner. A single LED array cast a bluish hue on them as Andy wrestled with the doorknob, an attempt to keep it shut.

"Oh, come on." He shook the buzz in his head and pushed her out of the way. Placing a hand on the wall, he pulled heat from the structure, cooling the small storage room by several degrees. The energy flowed into the metal jamb, welding a foot of the door shut. How he did it, he did not know. All he knew was that he was tired, and impatient, and too much had been kept from him.

He waved away the tang of red-hot steel. Andy stared, her jaw clenched, and swallowed.

"What the fuck is going on, Andy?"

"I'm sorry, we have no time. We have to get out of here."

"Stop the bullshit!" He no longer cared if they heard him out in the lobby. "I'm not going anywhere until you tell me what is going on."

"I can't. Not here."

"Listen to me," he hissed. "I've known you for what, three days? I've gotten sucker punched, dropped out of a penthouse, almost drowned, and now some very enthusiastic cops are trying to arrest me. And that was all because you stopped me from killing myself."

She stared at the ground.

"I think you sent me up to meet that madman—a madman who said he was your husband—because you wanted me to fail. So we are going nowhere until you tell me *what the hell* is going on."

"I told you. There is no hell."

"STOP THIS BULLSHIT!" The shout reverberated in the enclosed space, carrying every ounce of anger in his body.

And in an instant, Andy Vestal crumpled to the ground, shrieking in pain.

In a second, he knew. He saw everything in her: the twisting of her spine, the snap of her ribs, the pressure on her liver.

All of it exactly like the crush of pain he'd felt this afternoon, when Maxwell Salvatore had done the same to him.

He dropped to his knees. "Andy, I'm sorry! Oh my god I'm so sorry..."

She rolled onto her side, eyes shut, and caught her breath. Prospero tried his best to assist, which, given that he was terrified of making things worse, was of no help at all. He hovered next to her instead, his insides writhing with shame.

"Are you okay?"

Andy nodded and leaned against a metal shelf to catch her breath. Prospero looked away, unable to face her, focusing on not vomiting. He lost track of time as Andy's breath slowed, her gray eyes brimming with pain.

She looked tired, even more than a few days ago. With her short hair and piercing eyes, she looked exactly like Maxwell Salvatore's assistant.

"I guess you're ready now," she whispered.

"Nice of you to say that. I'm sorry I hurt you."

"I should have told you myself." She adjusted herself against a shelf holding buckets and cleaning materials. "That I was married to Maxwell."

"I know. He told me."

"For one hundred years."

It took him a moment to realize she was joking. "Wow, Andy, that must've been one hell of an anniversary."

He grinned, trying to make light of their situation—he'd almost broken her, after all—but Andy did not smile.

"Are you... serious?"

She nodded, gray eyes locked on his. He imagined an ocean of time—wars, plagues, revolutions—while a dour Andromeda Vestal stood unmoving, watching the world seethe past her.

"Ever wondered why we haven't found anyone out there, Prospero?"

"Andy, are you okay? Did you hit your head?" He craned his neck to look at her skull to see if she was bleeding. "You're making no sense."

She waved off the snipe. "Out there in the stars. Mathematics says the universe should be teeming with life. But it's silent. That silence is the Fermi Paradox. Ever wondered why?"

This was the stupidest possible conversation to have in a storage room in the middle of Tampa, hiding from three federal agents, after he'd fallen from a skyscraper, and almost killed someone.

Or perhaps it wasn't, because in an instant, he knew why she'd asked the question.

He crumpled onto the concrete and leaned against a shelf full of toilet paper. "Is that what you meant?" he murmured. "When you said..."

"Yes, Prospero. Some think we're alone because every other intelligent civilization seems to end up destroying itself."

"And Maxwell...?"

"Thinks humanity is on the same path."

His heart raced as the words spilled out. "A path to extinction?"

"Yes. And my former husband thinks he can stop that—by becoming a god."

CHAPTER 24

They huddled against the biting wind, watching the orange skyline. After a few minutes, they discovered their clothing was no match for the chill three hundred feet up. Prospero pulled up heat from the building to warm the roof, surrounding them in a swirl of comfort. Andy considered the feat with a grave stare and a terse nod.

Everything seemed easier by the minute. He'd bypassed the elevator by opening the doors, shunting the alarm, and energizing the circuit to zip them to the penthouse. All of this he did by touch. He had no idea how he knew, but he did, as if he could read past the surface of anything into the mechanics and order beneath. The sensation was akin to wearing those fancy new glasses that overlaid information, hiding the world behind. Wielding energy to manipulate his surroundings now came as easily as moving muscles to take a drink, or walk, or smile.

All of this after a fall that should've atomized him.

Andy no longer offered to help, and didn't need to. After a few doors and alarms, they climbed through the roof access, away from prying eyes. A mile away, the silhouette of Maxwell's building cut the night. Could he sense them, even now?

"Can we go back to the whole hundred-year marriage?"

Andy flashed a sad smile. "Sounds impossible, doesn't it? We'd been married ten years when Von Neumann and Wigner published their paper on the intersection between quantum mechanics and consciousness. We were already devotees of Eastern philosophy, and what they proposed blew our minds."

She rolled a pebble between her fingers. "We asked a lot of questions. Traveled to Austria. Maxwell — he went by Massimo then — tried to meet the luminaries. But the war turned everything into survival. So we trekked into what is now Tibet. Imagine our surprise when we found a village filled with people from all over the world, asking the same questions."

"A bunch of old people wondering why they married for a hundred years?"

She chuckled in silence and shook her head. "People who saw the world differently. Massimo loved the scientific foundation for what religions had tried for millennia to explain. The faithful gave it different names — Brahman, Dao, God. But at its heart, it was the same thing: the eternal consciousness of billions of souls."

"That sounds a lot like religion."

"Maybe. But the more time we spent with them, the more we changed. We didn't age, didn't get sick. After a few years, they shared more secrets."

"How not to kill each other after a century together?"

She shoved him with a thin smile. "For billions of years, the cosmos just was. Then life began, scattered among the stars. Some of it became intelligent, then conscious. The universe began to think about itself."

She gazed past the city to the dark sea. "For millennia we walked in the dark. Then came religion — our ancestors' attempt to name what they couldn't touch. They called it miraculous, divine. Later, science gave us a new language. Von Neumann and Wigner showed us we were always talking about the same thing."

"That miracles are just... applied science?"

"Applied science blurred by centuries, yes. We forgot that consciousness and the physical world are one. For thousands of years, we argued science versus magic, when they were never separate. Then quantum science revealed the truth as paradox. Von Neumann and Wigner were the first to say it: consciousness doesn't just observe the universe — it can *change* it."

His mind reeled, not at the idea, but at how obvious it now felt.

"Our awareness can shift reality. The least of us collapses a wave function in a school experiment. The rarest can create what others call miracles."

She squeezed his arm. "You did so with Professor Kinzer. Reordering a deck of cards against impossible odds. Nothing else explains it. It's part of the universe. Part of us."

"So is that what broke him?"

Her face fell. "One day Massimo asked if others out there had learned what we had. The silence of the night sky crushed him."

"The Fermi Paradox," Prospero muttered.

She nodded. "If life is common, where is it? He devoted his life to searching. The only explanation he could accept was that sparks of life elsewhere burned bright, then died. And that we're next."

"And Maxwell wants to stop that?"

"Not stop life. Stop choice. He believes free will dooms us — that every civilization destroys itself once it becomes conscious. So he wants to save humanity the only way he knows."

"By taking away choice."

"By dumbing us down until we don't want it. The tools he once built to search the stars now keep billions enslaved."

Prospero thought she looked immensely sad. "He's doing it to stave off extinction. Some might call that noble."

"Would you rather die free, or live as a slave?"

He exhaled. "So Maxwell wants to become a slave master."

"Not a slave master. A savior and a god."

He blew his breath out. "So what now?"

"You have to stop him."

Prospero glanced up at the stars and felt empty. "Stop him? Are you insane? He threw me out of a building."

"And you survived. How?"

"By not becoming meat sauce after a 500-foot fall?"

"You have a way with words, Prospero."

"And you have a way without them, Andy." He shook his head, then felt her hand on his arm.

"I just... knew," he whispered. "I wanted to be blown to the river... and it happened."

"It's working."

"No, it isn't! I don't even know what I did!"

"Do you think about every muscle you use to speak?"

He blinked, then shook his head.

"Sometimes you don't have to know. You just have to want. And believe." She hugged her knees, rocking as she stared at the horizon. "We hoped that if you met him, something would change. None of us imagined it would end this way. I'm sorry."

"We? This way?"

Andy nodded, then stood. "I'll explain, just not now. We have to go. Our ride awaits."

CHAPTER 25

They walked into the night through a service exit, past bored custodians engrossed in phones or glasses. Their ride, a rusted gray car, idled outside, lost in the city's bustle. The driver—about Prospero's age, fit and expressionless—nodded in recognition as they slid into the well-worn back seat. Without another word, the man drove off, heading north on the tollway.

"Are we going home?"

Andy shook her head. "We're going somewhere you can't be found."

"I promised Evangeline I'd be back."

"Things have changed, Prospero. Someone just tried to kill you."

He startled at the comment, stealing a glance at the driver, who glanced through the rearview mirror and said nothing.

"You're fine here. Among friends."

"Friends? What kind of friends?"

Andy offered a half-smile. "People who live quiet lives, who've sensed the world isn't quite what they've been told."

"The folks you met in the mountains? Are they like you... like him?"

She glanced in the rearview mirror. The driver gave the faintest nod.

"We're the ones who know where science and faith meet," he said, eyes fixed on the road, "and what's coming if he isn't stopped."

Silence settled over the car—heavy and unexpectedly comforting. Prospero wanted to say something—*thanks, good to meet you, how did you know*—but all he could think of was Evangeline.

"Please. I need to talk to her."

Andy nodded. As if on cue, the man held up what looked like a thin bar of soap.

"Make it quick," she said.

The object turned out to be a decades-old phone, European vintage. Prospero examined it and stopped.

"I don't know her number."

"You didn't memorize it? Is it on your phone?"

"Yeah, but... I landed in the river."

She grinned. "Good thing you know how to dry things."

He fished his own from his coat pocket. It was not much newer than the driver's, a choice made on purpose. Legacy technology remained the safest way to evade the ever-present infection of distraction that had taken his wife, and pretty much everyone else he knew.

Everyone except the people Andy knew... and Evangeline.

Unfortunately, trying to contact her would require using a waterlogged handset with a blank screen and a shorted battery. Forget rice: he'd need something far stronger to remove the water and dry the device.

Something he'd done this very night. Drying his clothes after his fall was only hours in his past.

"You don't mind?" He glanced at Andy, who shrugged in response.

He closed his eyes and placed a hand on the car door. The heat from the engine would provide more than enough energy for the task. All he had to do was focus, just as he'd focus on playing darts, or a move in chess, or threading a needle. Focusing on the outcome until his ears roared with that dull tone was the key.

When he opened his eyes, Andy had rolled down the window, waving away a cloud of mist. "Don't burn it!"

He pressed the ON button — he'd stolen a bit more from the engine to recharge the battery—and the phone beeped to life.

"You're getting better at this," Andy said.

He found her number and dialed. She answered on the second ring.

"Hello?"

"Evangeline, it's me."

"Where are you? What happened?"

"I'm fine. I'm ah—"

"Reels are going nuts, Prospero. Someone tried to kill Maxwell Salvatore. People are saying it's because of that headquarters he's building near Pasco. Are you okay?"

His stomach sank. "I'm fine. I heard about it. Must've happened afterwards and..."

"There were photos of a man who fell into the Hillsborough River." She paused, and Prospero's heart stopped. "He looked like you, Prospero. What is going on?"

Andy stared back.

"Evangeline, I'm going to lie low for tonight. There's a lot going on."

"Prospero, please come back. I'm worried about you, and this..."

"I'm sorry. I can't. People are looking for me."

A pause on the line, then a murmur. "You're with her, aren't you?"

A chill emptied his stomach. "Unfortunately, yes. Evangeline?"

"Yeah." Her whisper carried too much.

"I will be back soon. I promise. Please don't worry about me. About us."

"Are you *serious*? I'm not worried about that. I'm worried that she's crazy and setting you up for..." She didn't finish. Prospero went hollow, imagining her holding back terror.

"As soon as all this is over, I promise I'll write you another poem."

"You think I'm going to let you?"

"Evangeline, please. I was at the wrong place at the wrong time, and now people are looking for me. I will come back. I promise."

The handset hissed with silence.

"I miss you," she whispered.

"Miss you back."

He wanted to tell her so much more. Instead, he finished the call and looked outside, hoping the storm would abate. The car, he realized, was both ruse and cover. Maxwell could harness the forces of nature, but still had to follow them. A rolling metal box with sonic and electric noise was perfect camouflage against someone who could read the faint signatures of a thousand minds.

They meandered through endless exurbs north of the

university, arriving at a squat concrete house in a forgotten neighborhood, the kind where sandy, sunbaked yards hid behind chain-link fences. Decades ago, children would've played in the sunshine, protected from speeding traffic. The neighborhoods, forgotten as the city became its own suburb, still sported homes smaller than the garages housing the vehicles of the newly rich.

The man nodded as Andy stepped out of the car and knocked on the door. A few moments later, she waved at Prospero to come in.

He stepped out of the car, and finding the silence unbearable, whispered, "Thanks for the ride."

"Good luck." The man's gaze seared into his mind. "Remember what you've lived."

Then he sped off without another word.

Amber light lit the concrete pathway in soft shapes as Prospero entered and closed the door behind him. An unmistakable aura — or the earthy scent of wood—caught him by surprise.

"Mister Jones." Devdan Kinzer, looking older than one day ago, clasped his hands over his heart.

"Professor. I don't know what to—"

Then the old man embraced him, and wept.

CHAPTER 26

It was quite difficult to be angry at a weeping octogenarian. He tried his best to scowl at Kinzer and Andy, but failed at the task.

"You set me up," Prospero murmured.

"No, Mister Jones." Kinzer stepped back and wiped his eyes. "We never expected this."

"This?" Prospero stepped back to examine their surroundings. A warm light spilled from the door of the squat concrete home. "The world's richest man is also some... magician who almost killed me. And you didn't know that?"

Kinzer crossed his arms and stared at a threadbare rug. He seemed stuck in the same past as the house: old and forgotten, but steadfast against the whims of encroaching insanity.

"What were you expecting when you sent me there? That Salvatore was going to just talk and play nice?"

"Actually," Andy demurred, "that's exactly what we hoped."

Kinzer nodded. "We hoped that when he met you, he'd realize he was not alone. Not the only one who..."

"The only one who what?"

"Who shares your talents, Prospero." Andy crossed her arms and stared. "What we—I had hoped, knowing my husband—was that he'd understand he wasn't the only one. There was someone his equal who saw the world differently. And when he saw that, he'd consider another path."

"Someone who could make him see the truth," Kinzer added.

His ears rang in the silence. "No. You wanted him to believe I could stop him."

"That's putting things in a different—"

"No," Prospero snapped. "You thought that only someone like me could stop him. Didn't you? Except you didn't tell me." He paced the room, trying to run his fingers through his hair, again finding only stubble.

Kinzer and Andy turned to each other in apparent confession.

"There's no one else like you," Kinzer said.

Prospero closed his eyes and counted. This was not the time for maudlin pep talks. "I know we are all unique, but what I'm saying is—"

"There hasn't been anyone like you in a thousand years, Prospero Jones."

He blinked once, twice, ten times. "What are you saying?"

Kinzer ambled to a fabric couch, faded with age, and sank into the cushions. He seemed lost on the couch, blending into an old gingham blanket frayed with use. His spindly legs reminded Prospero of a baby bird taking first steps. Andy sat down across from him and waited.

"When I was a younger man," Kinzer said, "I was obsessed with patterns. Not numbers, not data—human patterns. Points in time where something... someone... disrupted the arc of history. Every so often, a person appears who is so deeply entangled with those who came before, it's as if the weight of past generations flows through them. They change everything. They always do."

"Sounds like you're talking about messiahs," Prospero added.

"Call them what you want," Kinzer replied. "But humanity calls them something else: impossible."

"Every thousand years?" Prospero sat on the armrest of a chair, arms crossed. "That's very convenient, Professor. A bit too anthropomorphic. Sounds like prophecy, not science."

"The first eleven digits of pi, in seconds, is a number equal to about nine hundred and ninety-six years. A curious and inexplicable resonance, one our conscious minds struggle to decipher." Kinzer rubbed his knuckles, avoiding Prospero's gaze.

"It isn't perfect, by any stretch. More of a buildup, like pressure beneath a tectonic plate. For a thousand years, the consciousness of the billions who have come before has accumulated. And then—very rarely—someone is born who can carry it all. They don't choose it. They don't train for it. They just are."

Andy nodded. "And when that happens, the world shifts."

"Last time it happened," Kinzer said, "the world believed the end was near. Visions. Signs. Whole empires converted or collapsed. Some called it the millennium panic. Others called it divine intervention. Now we know it was more than that. It has always been a phase transition, where consciousness can bend reality. Like water turning to ice, then back."

"Is Maxwell this... person?"

They stared back in silence.

"Wait, no. You're saying... it's me?"

"You may be," Andy said. "And so is Maxwell. And the world will follow only one of you."

Prospero stood. "Follow? What do you mean?"

"Maxwell promises salvation through submission. You offer the light to that darkness: the terror and elation of free will, with no guarantees."

"How do you know this?"

She leveled her gaze at him. "Those people we met, the ones who showed us what lies beyond. They meditated for centuries, hoping that person would appear in their lifetimes." She stopped, as if to cement in his mind that she'd keep no more secrets. "I was unprepared for that person to be my husband. And eternally grateful to discover he was not the only one."

The world tilted, and he grabbed onto a chair to keep from flying off. "I was ready to die three days ago. I couldn't keep my life together. And now you're telling me I'm some... cosmic tuning fork?"

"Not a tuning fork." Kinzer gazed up and smiled. "You are far beyond that, Mister Jones. You've both already bent energy, probability, and matter. All through free will."

"And Maxwell believes he can save the world by taking it away," Andy added. "But you—you're the proof of what humanity can achieve when it embraces it."

Prospero turned away. He tapped a fist against the back of a chair. "You keep talking like this is a gift. Like I asked for it."

"No one does," Kinzer said. "But in retrospect, it had to be you."

Prospero stared out the window. Trees swayed in the gentle ocean breeze. The world moved and thrived without him, without them, without Maxwell and a hundred thousand billion souls.

Three days ago, he'd planned to end it all. Now he was being asked to save the world.

And all he wanted was to tell Evangeline about it. The gulf between them yawned as wide as the chasm of possibilities ahead, and he teetered on its edge.

"I'm not ready," he muttered.

"No one ever is," Andy replied. "But it's happening. You're not alone anymore, Prospero. And you are the only one who can stop him."

He turned away from the gnawing awareness that Andy was right. What good was saving the world if he lost Evangeline?

CHAPTER 27

"Ready?"

Prospero nodded and led Andy into the dark, silent center of Mullet Cove.

He'd slept in fits after Kinzer's revelation, staring at the ceiling of the lone bedroom, waking to find Andy curled up on the couch. Kinzer was gone.

"We don't need to risk you any longer," Andy replied to his silent question over instant coffee. "You know everything we know."

The rest of the day dragged on. He managed a quick call to Evangeline, who did not answer. If Andy was to be believed, he could not blame her. Andy remarked that it was for the best, and they whiled away the day reading books and eating packaged noodles. The faded pages of paperbacks felt comforting: delightfully archaic in a world brimming with manufactured distraction. He devoured half of a provocative book about alternate history—where the Great War had ended differently—when Andy roused him from the reverie and informed him they'd better get going.

Now they stepped out onto a dark street in Mullet Cove, the forgotten neighborhoods of every beach town in Florida. Far from the sand and close to traffic, blasted by sun and littered with the detritus of big-box stores, these were the places tourists avoided. But locals knew better: these streets were the heartbeat of these towns, where curious souls could escape the forced shell game of vacationers.

Main Street hummed in the darkness, as if the town itself recovered from a day of sun and life and noise. A procession of breweries—Mullet Cove had more than its share—were shuttered on weekday evening. The past days were a blur: waking up in Evangeline's bed, the revelations with Kinzer, discovering a past with Evangeline he'd never imagined, only to end in a bitter parting. Then Maxwell's attempt on his life, his inexplicable survival, before evading the cops and watching the sunset with a friend he'd almost killed.

Had it been only days since he'd first kissed Evangeline? Everything moved fast, but when she was near, the world slowed, and made sense. He thought of her eyes and her smile —open, honest, endless—and struggled to imagine how he could ever tell her how much his life had changed.

Evangeline's second-floor apartment overlooked Main Street —both a remnant of the town's heyday and hope for its future. Prospero led Andy through a back alley to avoid prying eyes.

He knew something was wrong when he saw Evangeline's door spilling light onto the railing. He motioned to Andy to stay back, pulling kilotons of energy from the building and ground. If anyone had dared hurt her... he raced up the steps, awash in the roar of energy. He shoved the door open, turned his clothing to armor, and blazed the lights on, bathing the apartment in an LED glow.

Nothing. Someone had forced the door open, but taken nothing. He returned his clothes to normal and checked the rest of the studio. Her bed lay undisturbed; her flip-phone was nowhere.

Evangeline was gone.

He stepped out of the apartment and noticed Andy looking at something hidden from view.

"She's not here," Prospero hissed.

A slight figure sat up from the stairwell shadows. Angie, the coffee shop manager, placed a finger on her lips, shivering from inside an oversize hoodie.

They drove in silence to a little development a few blocks off the water, less than a mile from his apartment. Angie's house, a rickety two-story bungalow, stood back from the bayou in an old neighborhood now overtaken by rich snow-birds. They parked in the tiny driveway and snuck up the back stairs.

He felt her before Angie opened the door.

"Oh my god!" Evangeline sprang into Prospero's embrace, shaking with quiet sobs. She held his face, eyes sparkling with tears. "What is happening?"

"I don't know. But I'm so glad you're safe."

Angie closed the door behind them, bolted the door, then shut the blinds. George, her husband, met them with a bleary-eyed handshake.

"So what happened to your apartment?"

Evangeline squeezed his hands. "Guys in tactical gear showed up at the shop this morning, looking for me. Angie let me know, and Bobby hid me at his bar for a few hours."

"They broke into Eve's place." Angie curled herself inside the hoodie, a tiny ball lost on a green sofa, swallowing a tiny sob. "I gave Eve our key and went to her place when you both arrived."

Evangeline squeezed his hand. Her eyes had lost their light. "What is happening? Are you in trouble?"

Prospero swayed. How could he ever explain?

"Someone tried to kill him." Andy's voice cut the silence. "Then tried to frame him for the attack."

Angie and Evangeline stared in silence. "The news said someone tried to kill Maxwell Salvatore."

He was about to reply when Andy cut him off. "We can't share much more. But that's not what happened."

"Oh my god..." Evangeline held fast, crying into his shoulder. He closed his eyes, focusing on her embrace and committing her honeysuckle scent to memory. He wanted to share every memory, every part of himself, with her.

But what could he say? That a warlock desperate to enslave humanity tried to kill him, but he'd survived...because both he and the madman were the same?

Evangeline pulled back and wiped her nose. "I'm so sorry about yesterday morning... I was angry, and mean, and you didn't deserve any of that, and—"

He raised her chin, marveling at her inexplicable perfection. "You were right. About everything. As usual."

"About him?"

He nodded.

She scrunched her nose in a wet grin and buried her face in his shoulder.

"Right about what?" Angie asked.

"Maxwell Salvatore," Evangeline mumbled from somewhere on his chest. "Total asshole."

Angie took a sip of water. "You left for that meeting, and suddenly everything went crazy."

"Your meeting was with Maxwell Salvatore?" George looked up from behind a refrigerator door. "Dude who built that tech campus outside of town?"

Andy shifted, glaring to catch Prospero's attention. Evangeline replied with a disgusted "Yeah."

George tapped his glasses and stiffened. After a few moments, he disappeared into the bedroom.

Prospero tried to focus on Evangeline's warmth against his chest. The sound of drawers opening and shutting seemed a strange backdrop for their reunion.

Angie must've noticed the intrusion into their moment. "Everything okay back there?"

"I'm all good," George answered, followed by something big scraping on the floor.

Angie sighed and rolled her eyes. "I'm sorry. He's adorable, but he's a slob."

"I got your letter," Evangeline whispered.

"What letter?" He froze. Three days ago he'd left his house, planning to end everything. He'd left behind very little, including something that now seemed misplaced.

She leaned back to look him in the eye. "Were you really going to... do it?"

He pulled her close, fresh out of anything to say.

"Prospero, why? And why did you leave me all of this?"

"I'll... I'll explain later. I promise."

She rested her head between his neck and shoulder, and nodded.

Angie stared at them in silence until it became uncomfortable. "Why did that guy want to meet with you?"

Andy shot him a worried glance, but keeping secrets no longer worked. Especially when the secret involved getting launched out a skyscraper window without a parachute, or hiding the fact that a botched suicide had changed his life in the most bizarre fashion.

"Not sure, but he didn't seem too excited about—"

George burst out of the bedroom, leveling a rifle at Prospero's head. "Don't move."

Angie shrieked. "Gio! What the fuck is wrong with you! Put that down!"

"I said, don't move," George barked. His wild eyes belied a steady aim.

Evangeline turned, placing Prospero behind her. "Georgie, what the hell are you doing?"

George's eyes darted from Angie to Prospero, but the rifle didn't waver. "I'm sorry, Eve, but your friend is a fugitive. He tried to kill Salvatore. It's been on the feeds all day."

"What are you talking about, Gio!" Angie stepped forward, hands open. "Look at them! Put that fucking thing down!"

"He parachuted from a skyscraper. He's no amateur, babe, and we won't be accessories to an assassination attempt. Both of you, please sit. Eve, you can join him. They're coming."

"Coming? Who is coming?" Evangeline demanded. "Georgie, you are freaking me out and —"

"I said, join him!" George swung the rifle towards her, and everything changed.

The apartment's lights dimmed and flickered, and the top half of George's rifle crumbled in a pile of bluish dust.

"What the..."

Prospero ripped heat from the room and slammed George against the wall. Fog burst around them as the temperature dropped, the windows spidering with frost. Angie shrieked as plaster rained down.

"He got to you, right?" Prospero hissed. He felt the iron ripping from George's blood, the calcium flying from his bones. In seconds, they'd rip from his body, shredding him to—

"Pete, let him go."

The voice startled him. He stemmed the onslaught and turned to find Andy, the only calm person in the room, staring him down. "Don't be like him."

"Like him? This little fucking snitch deserves it!"

"No," she murmured. "Like Maxwell."

The words gutted him. That was not him. Could never be him...

He released his focus, and George collapsed, gasping for breath. His broken glasses fell to the ground.

Angie leapt to her husband's aid, brushing debris from his face. Prospero barely heard her yelling through the ringing in his ears. One more second, and he would've ended George's life.

Evangeline knelt by the rifle, staring at the cracked wall, her face blank. She rubbed the powder between her fingers and locked eyes with Prospero.

"This is why you met Kinzer. Wasn't it?" Her breathing sped up, shallower each moment, as she reached inside her shorts pocket. She held the bismuth pebble and stared with wide eyes. Her lips quivered when she spoke.

"Was... *this* what you were trying to tell me? Please tell me this is not you..."

His ears rang; whether from the effort or from betrayal he could not tell, enough to hide the soft padding of footsteps outside.

Then the door burst open, something sharp popped into his back, and his world ended.

CHAPTER 28

Sand, heavy and dark.

Then light.

Someone next to him.

Evangeline? No. Jeanine?

Andy?

Did he die—again?

"Where am I?" He tried to speak, but nothing came out.

Don't move.

The thought confused him. Why was he talking to himself?

It took him a moment to realize he was hearing Andy's voice. He opened his eyes a sliver. She sat across from him in the back of an expansive vehicle, staring outside as unfamiliar streetlights whizzed past.

For his part, Prospero slumped against the door with all the style of a sack of potatoes, his wrists and ankles bound, skin raw where zip ties dug into his flesh.

I can't move, he thought.

I clamped your mouth and muscles shut.

What a friend would do, he thought. He tried to laugh, but in his current state, the effort resulted in something like a spasm. His heart raced in a burning chest.

Don't fight. They'll do it again

Do what?

What they used to put you down.

Did it wear off?

Her eyes flicked to the men in front.

No, I tried to speed up your metabolism.

I'm alive?

They'll sedate you again if you move.

He wanted to scream, to stretch and tear free, but Andy remained impassive.

Where's Evangeline?

Car behind us.

Is she okay?

Andy inhaled, then nodded on the exhale.

Shit. How long had he been out? It was dark outside, and Andy had mentioned his metabolism. So it had been only hours since George the idiot had tried to shoot him. Which meant it was way past his bedtime. And that these people weren't—

They're with Maxwell, he heard her say, as if she was reading his thoughts, which she definitely was.

He squeezed his eyes shut, still feigning unconsciousness, and let his mind expand. One driver. Gunman in the passenger seat. Two more in the seat behind them, armed with guns and needles.

Every single one tense, focused on him, and ready to pounce.

But they hadn't yet. And in an instant, he knew why.

Evangeline. Maxwell Salvatore had found his leverage.

The car slowed and turned, not a good sign. He felt the bewilderment in Andy's mind before she could think anything at him and opened his thoughts to let her listen.

Hold on.

What are you going to do?

Hold on.

He pulled with all his might, draining all heat energy from the engine. The car sputtered, gently at first, then abruptly. Lights inside flickered as tires screeched as they jerked to an abrupt stop.

"What the fuck?" the driver barked.

The men behind them leaned into their seatbelts, growling in bewilderment. For an instant, Prospero feared they might jab him. Before the confusion abated, they heard the following car grind to a halt behind them. A breath later, the doors flung open. Prospero felt the hard metal of guns pointed at them. Through a slit in his vision he saw Andy lean back, eyes wide.

"What happened?"

The driver slammed the steering wheel. "Car just died. Battery?"

"Don't think so." A man yanked Andy out of the car as his teammate clicked a device, raising his hand. "Take him out again."

More sedatives. He needed to do something. *Now.*

He felt the roar in his mind as heat unleashed in a barrage of blinking lights and fried watches. The surrounding men shook their heads, stunned for an instant.

"What the fuck...?"

"My glass is down."

"So's my phone."

"And my watch."

Someone yelled behind them. "Car just died! Someone call the boss!"

He had little strength left in him after the pulse. Manipulating this much energy was much harder when you were sedated and bound. Another jab was inconceivable if they were to survive and see Evangeline again.

Then a voice. "Hey where are you going?"

He sensed Andy walking away, calm and deliberate. Was she leaving him? Trading him for something?

The crack of a rifle answered the question.

"He's awake! Grab her!"

Everything fell apart. Someone pushed the seat forward and ran toward the now-sprinting Andy. The other guy leaned over the seat and pushed something against Prospero's skin.

The man pulled back, examining the injector. "What the—"

Prospero's teeth chattered, colder than he'd ever felt in his life. Apparently, his body held enough energy to transmute a needle's worth of metal into silicon. Now he lay frozen and still, incapable of movement.

Unless...

A roaring wave crashed into him, warming him back to life. He was exhausted and tired, but alive and breathing.

He sat up, woozy from the sedatives, spent from manipulating so much heat. A waxy face stared from the back seat, eyes frozen in terror by his will.

He lurched out of the van, trying to focus on the men running after Andy, wondering if he'd held back enough to not kill a man.

CHAPTER 29

Stop. Please.

He shut his eyes, praying Andy could hear him. A quarter mile away, shuffling past a gas station, he felt her slow down. She stopped and turned back.

"On the ground!"

He was about to think a warning to her when something clicked behind him. The bloom of an electric charge...

He fell to the ground as two delicate wires hissed above him, then descended like falling leaves. Whoever trained these assholes was good. Just enough time...

He yanked heat from the pavement and turned his clothes stiff. A heartbeat later, two more darts slammed into him, ricocheting off. He looked up as another gunman closed in, reloading. A second later, he raised his weapon and fired.

These rounds hit him like a hammer, cracking something wet inside him.

Those hadn't been tranquilizer rounds. The roar of the assault rifle threatened to split his mind open.

"Drop your weapon!"

What the fuck were these idiots saying? He had no weapon — not yet, at least. He flattened himself against the ground, the stiff clothing digging into his ribs, when the world erupted.

Automatic fire ripped through the night as supersonic metal zipped inches above him. He grasped at the pebbled asphalt and shunted all his energy into his clothes, hoping whatever madman was shooting would not aim at his head.

Then, silence.

Andy?

"Stay down!"

The voice was not directed at him. He turned to glance at his attackers. They sprawled on the ground, their weapons scattered. Over them stood a familiar figure, wielding a military rifle with unnerving ease, speaking in his unmistakable voice.

"This is Special Agent Miles Dalton requesting immediate assistance at Clearwater Airpark. We have two armed subjects in custody."

Armed? Prospero wasn't armed.

Dalton's eyes found his. The young agent opened his trigger hand, almost in supplication. *Stay down, please.*

Prospero could read it—not in the young man's mind, but in his demeanor, his actions, his breathing, his heart rate. All somehow understandable, despite their prior introduction.

Brooks—the young woman he'd slammed into the car—cuffed the shooters, then sprinted past. Prospero craned his neck as Andy walked toward them, hands raised. The pursuers in the following car were long gone.

He let the fabric loosen, hoping Dalton wouldn't shoot him in the back, when someone knelt beside him.

"Please don't move. You are coming with us."

Dalton's face glowed blue from the pulsing lights of a cruiser. Leaning on his own assault weapon, he helped Prospero to his feet.

"I'm hoping you don't think I caused this, too."

"You are a witness to a Federal assault," Dalton hissed. "These two men fired on agents in the course of carrying out their duties. You're coming with us." He pulled Prospero in close and hissed. "Please."

"You gonna shoot me again?"

"Shut up. I'm trying to help you."

"There's a young woman in that SUV," Prospero whispered. His ribs protested the effort.

Dalton grabbed him and flashed a badge at a pair of sheriffs exiting a white police cruiser.

"Special Agent Miles Dalton. We have jurisdiction."

"Sorry, buddy." The sheriff's armor strained over his belly. "Need a magistrate release. And the reason you're carrying weapons on my turf. We're the ones who have jurisdiction. "

Agent Brooks, sporting a blooming welt on her cheek, shoved a tablet at him. "Here."

The two cops scrolled, scowled, then pulled out their weapons. "You have the right to remain silent..."

The litany was not meant for him. Two sheriffs cuffed the men on the ground, talking into their mikes as the night blew up in lights.

Prospero counted four trucks, two cruisers, and a fire truck all bearing down on them from every direction. He was about to crack a joke about a slow night when Dalton shoved him towards a familiar black car.

Young Nora sat behind the wheel, glaring straight ahead. She'd left an impressive dent on the vehicle the last time they'd met. He tried to catch her eye in a sheepish offer of truce, but she avoided his gaze. He couldn't blame her. Trust was a long way in the future.

He slid into the back seat opposite Andy. The doors closed with a heavy thunk, bathing them in silence, when a familiar voice whispered behind them.

"What is going on?"

He spun to face her.

"Oh my god, Evangeline!" Her perfect face had turned ashen. He was about to whisper something in reply when Agent Nora Brooks, perhaps in a fit of revenge, floored the accelerator and the vehicle peeled away.

"Where are we going?" Prospero asked once the g-forces subsided.

Dalton turned from the passenger seat, studying him.

"Did you just freeze a man?"

CHAPTER 30

The SUV tore down darkened streets, taking corners too fast and screeching tires on the pavement. Agent Nora Brooks drove like a maniac, and Prospero wondered if she was getting back at him.

He braced himself against the door with each turn. Evangeline had joined them, wedged between him and Andy, holding onto any available handhold. Andy grasped the handle over the door, a faint smile on her lips.

Sitting behind Nora, he could not see her face, nor could he escape Agent Dalton's severe gaze, split between him and Andy.

"You haven't answered my question, Mister Jones."

He glanced at Evangeline, who stared back with wide eyes.

"It's been a few manic days, Agent Dalton. Just a trick."

Dalton nodded, as if expecting the evasion. He considered Prospero for a long pause before pinching the bridge of his nose and letting out a dramatic sigh.

"I want to make this crystal clear, Mister Jones. I am going on a flyer here, and if you let me down, you're going to be in a world of hurt. Do I make myself clear?"

"Am I under arrest?"

"You'll be under arrest again if you don't answer my damn question. Are we *clear*?"

Every hint of kindness had left Dalton's voice. Prospero stared at the floor and nodded before gazing back at the young man. "I'm clear. I didn't do anything to that man. I just... head-butted him."

Brooks and Dalton glanced at each other. "He was shivering," Nora Brooks said in a monotone. "Could barely move."

"He's not dead, then."

Dalton twisted into a smirk. "Of *course* he's not dead. But he was shivering like he'd seen a ghost."

"Why are you helping us?"

Nora glanced in the rearview mirror, eyebrows knit in something like curiosity. "It appears Mister Salvatore has been less than forthcoming," she replied.

"The Department had a bad feeling about Salvatore for years, but nothing stuck," Dalton continued. "And then you threw in that line about his daughter. So we checked her out."

Dalton's voice cut through the roar of the tires. "Neither Salvatore nor the woman he claims is his daughter exists on paper. No records. Nothing."

Prospero flashed to the young woman at the lobby desk — blank eyes, a mechanical smile. At the time he thought it was those damn glasses. Now he wondered if she was even alive.

"See?" Evangeline hissed. "I told you he was trouble!"

Dalton pressed on. "He's raised hundreds of millions. Perfectly legal. But not once has his name appeared in a single ledger, a single filing. Every dollar runs through shell companies and trusts, all of them airtight. But he's now*here*. A ghost in the machine."

Nora glanced at them through the mirror. "Imagine opening a box you've tracked for months — and finding nothing inside."

"That's not surprising," Andy muttered, almost to herself.

Evangeline leaned forward. "You can't move money without a trail. Not even if you're the richest man alive."

Dalton twisted in his seat. The dashboard lights cast his face in pale blue. "The trails are there. It's their beginnings we can't find. The only way that works is if he meets every investor face-to-face. No contracts, no filings. Just quiet conversations... and a lot of coercion."

"A conglomerate as big as his?" Evangeline shook her head. "That would take decades."

"More than decades," Dalton said. "Our analysts think it's a century of work done in the span of Apex's life." His gaze flicked to Andy. "No one does that in one lifetime."

Prospero's ribs ached as he leaned back. *A hundred years.* Andy's stare caught his, wide and unblinking.

"And it gets worse," Dalton said. "Those people with the guns? They weren't security personnel. Every one of them was a private citizen."

Prospero leaned closer. "What do you mean?"

"Salvatore was connecting through their glasses. Their handsets. They're zealots on a leash. An army he doesn't have to pay, ready to jump in at a moment's notice."

Prospero saw George's face in the blur — the twitching hand, the steady voice that hadn't been his own, a far cry from the idealistic soldier that Angie adored. Evangeline stole a glance at him, mouth wide in disbelief.

"That's why you're coming with us," Dalton finished.

Andy broke the silence. "Where?"

"Safe house. At least for the night. Ms. See will go with our Tampa police liaison. They'll put her up at a hotel for the evening."

For a moment, Prospero hoped Evangeline would protest, and stay with them. He turned, his mind on fire, to say anything. Evangeline sat back and stared ahead.

The sprawl of horse country north of Tampa unfolded into long stretches of pine forest and darkness. A nervous quiet descended upon them, as if the night had swallowed the insanity of the night, and left it to fester.

They turned into an access-controlled neighborhood, with townhomes laid out in a pleasant fashion around wooded lakes. He'd never been to places like this, perhaps because he hated the state with all his might. That changed the day he met Evangeline. He squeezed her hand, but she didn't squeeze back.

Nora parked in an empty back lot, then disappeared for a few minutes. No one dared speak. A few minutes later, she tapped Dalton's window.

"Clear."

They entered a second-floor apartment and closed the darkness behind them. The apartment, decorated in a mono-chrome palette, exuded all the vitality of the bedding section of a home goods store. A few items of furniture, spartan and minimalistic, showed little wear. Nora showed them their rooms — two bedrooms, two baths — the location of the panic button, and where the outside cameras pointed. They could tap a button on the kitchen tablet for immediate help.

"Try not to open the door," Nora explained. "The windows and doors have mesh. You can't get a signal out except for those."

"Flip phones won't work?"

"Nothing will work," Dalton replied. "You're in a cell phone bubble. Best we can do with someone who has a knack for finding you."

This felt more like a prison than a refuge. The air, sharp and sterile, carried no scent of anything alive. An air handler hummed in the background, a white noise that grated instead of soothed. Even though he felt exhausted to the bone, he wondered how he'd sleep tonight. The concern about Evangeline would keep him awake until dawn.

"We'll be in touch early tomorrow. Get some rest. We need some as well."

Evangeline surprised them with a whisper. "Can we... have a minute?"

Dalton glanced at his watch. "Make it quick."

Andy gestured to the rooms, as if saying, "Be my guest," and they closed the door behind them until only a sliver of the world remained.

He reached out for her hand, but she grabbed his wrists.

"Why were you going to kill yourself?"

CHAPTER 31

For a moment, he thought of lying. Despite the insanity, coming clean with the one person who meant everything terrified him the most.

"You sent me a suicide note, Prospero. You were leaving me your books and your royalties. What were you going to do?"

He flopped onto the bed and held his face in his fists.

"And what the heck happened at Angie's apartment? You stared at Geo, and then he slammed himself against the wall. The room turned to ice. What is going on?"

He stared at the carpet—industrial, dark gray with flecks of black—and let the silence envelop him.

"Prospero, please. Talk to me."

He tried to speak for an age until the torrent burst. "Something is changing, Evangeline. My wife left me. My daughter died before she could live. I have two adopted children whom I've never met. I lost my job, my house, everything. So I decided to kill myself."

He stopped at the crushing, overwhelming failure, and squeezed his eyes shut to push away the shame.

"I woke up thinking I was dead, and found Andy in my apartment. Telling me things I didn't know but could somehow understand. Next thing I knew, my world broke apart."

"Broke apart?"

He nodded. "Remember when we were chatting at Bobby's? When you told me about the observer effect, and the different interpretations? Everything Kinzer talked about? For some reason, I can now... I don't even know how to explain."

She reached into her pocket and produced the pebble. "This?"

He nodded.

"Why didn't you tell me?"

"Tell you what? That I wanted to kill myself, that some witch rescued me, that now I can change limestone into metal, and that I think I'm going insane?"

She surprised him by sitting down and squeezing his knee. "All of that. Yes."

"Can you imagine me dumping all of this on you?"

"Why wouldn't you?" she whispered in reply.

He shook his head. "Because it makes no sense. Because you'd think I'm crazy. I'm a washed-up failure. You're beautiful and young. I'm an old guy with a crush telling you a fantastic story to seek your attention."

"Would you *please* stop with that?" She slapped her thighs, then clenched her fists. "I'm almost thirty, Prospero. You're just over forty. This isn't a May-December thing. It's like a June-July thing. You could be my older brother. Please don't push me away because of something you imagine. Just... please let me in."

He wanted to lay his head on her shoulder, but teetered instead. "I wanted to end it. Instead, I get a curse. I don't know what is happening to me. I don't know what is happening, *period.*"

"I don't know, either. But I want to help."

Their eyes met. She could somehow convey every feeling in the cosmos through her gaze. Today she'd been pursued, kidnapped, witnessed a shooting, and spirited to a hiding place. All because of him, and whatever insane reality he now controlled.

And despite all of that, *she* was the one trying to comfort *him.* He was profoundly lucky to have been born in her world. And utterly undeserving of her attention.

"I'm putting you in danger, Evangeline."

She shook her head. "Let me tell you how I see this. You've been kind, and respectful, and understanding, when the rest of the world has been cruel and vindictive and blind."

Her lips quivered. "You're even doing it now. The world is coming after you, everything is changing, and you're still more worried about me. That is the exact opposite of dangerous."

He was about to reply when she squeezed his hand. "We have both led lives that didn't work out like we wanted. And now, against all reason, despite every past failure, despite how crazy this world becomes, we've found each other. Don't you think that is a miracle?"

"Evangeline, we've only just met, and now my life—"

She squeezed his hand to stop him. "We haven't just met. I've known you for over a year. And maybe you didn't notice, but you have always been special."

He glanced at her, racing to understand.

"Do you have any idea what my life is like when you're not in it?"

"A bunch of guys hitting on you at the coffee shop?"

She rolled her eyes. "Ever since you left me those flowers, I smile when you walk in. Everyone else is a drone in their little world. Not you."

"I'm just someone who cares for you. Probably inappropriately."

She smiled for the first time since the world had turned. "I'm very thankful that you were so inappropriate the other night. You still owe me some poems."

He tried to smile back, but remembered the terror in her eyes when he pinned George against the wall. "Something inside me is changing."

She stiffened. "About me?"

"No, whatever... *this* is, scares me." He stood up and paced the bedroom. "I turned limestone into something radioactive. I survived a fall from a skyscraper. I almost crushed George." He stared at the ground. "I almost killed Luke."

"What are you talking about?"

"When he badmouthed you at Bobby's. That wasn't a seizure. That was me."

"I... don't understand."

He placed a hand on the wall, pulling energy from the building's heat, shunting it to the electrical system. The bedroom lamp and ceiling fixtures flickered. Evangeline sat back, clutching herself.

"That, a thousand times over. Then you patched me up, and we ended up together. I never told you the truth."

She stared back. "He tried to assault me. Then he hit you!"

"I made a mistake."

"Made in self-defense." She reached for his hands. "And maybe he did have a seizure. Prospero, you are not going insane. Whatever is going on... I want to be there with you."

"What if I make another mistake? What if I don't know what I'm doing?"

"None of us knows what we are doing. How do you think I felt, sharing everything with you? Do you think that was a mistake?"

He shook his head. "Being with you is the only thing I've done right. And now I'm terrified I'll hurt you."

She held his hand. "You know what really scares me? Thinking that in this insane world, I'm going to face life alone. That every choice I've made might lead me away from happiness and fulfillment. For three years, the more I learned, the more desperate I became. And then you popped into my life, and your only wish is that I'm happy."

Her hair cascaded over her face as she shook her head. "What scares me is that the past three days had been the happiest of my life. I shared all of myself with you. And I'm terrified that all of it might go away because you won't let me in."

He pulled her into an embrace. He wanted to tell her the impossible—*I love you, from the moment I saw you*—but it would never be right. So he remained silent until she pulled back and pulled wisps of hair from her wet cheeks.

He wanted to kiss her right there, to thank her for being the most perfect being in all of creation, to tell her that none of his life had made sense until he first saw her smile.

But he said nothing. What was he thinking? That he could tell her he loved her, that he'd give his life up for hers, that when they were apart a part of him died—and expect that to make everything better?

No. The moment she learned about the real him, she'd walk away for good.

"Prospero, I...." She held his face, staring into his soul with blazing eyes. "I... should go."

They shared an awkward embrace, and then she was gone. Evangeline See, the center of his life and owner of his soul, the most perfect being ever, turned and walked out the door.

He stayed back for a moment, suddenly aware of the ceiling fan barely moving air. Gray walls stared back, a blank canvas where he could replay every single thing he should've said and didn't. The roar of silence engulfed him, leaving behind the sting of regret.

He stepped out of the room in time to see Evangeline walk out with Nora Brooks. Neither looked back.

Miles Dalton interrupted his thoughts. "You'll be okay for tonight?"

"We will," Andy replied. "Thank you for helping us."

They locked the door behind them, leaving a cloying silence to flood the room.

"You okay?" Andy crossed her arms against the chill, her face knit with concern.

"Yeah. Fine."

"Want to talk about what happened?"

He shook his head.

"Evangeline is brilliant, and empathetic," she whispered. "She is quite special. But what you are becoming, what you are learning, is hard for anyone to understand. It will take time to accept. And that includes you."

She surprised him with a hug, then disappeared into her room. Prospero plopped down on the bed where, minutes before, he'd screwed everything up with Evangeline. In the midst of the crisis that should've brought them together, silence had driven them apart.

Every decision he'd taken had failed. The framed degree

shoved into a cardboard box. The crib he built for a daughter who didn't live. A marriage gone bitter. Signing adoption papers for children he'd never meet. The bills piling so high, he no longer opened them.

A house emptied, room by room, until everyone forgot his name.

And now, the one person who made the world bearable had walked away, because he was too afraid to let her see what he'd become.

The silence pressed in, heavy and merciless. He tried to imagine one moment, just one, where he had chosen differently, where he hadn't failed.

None came.

What if Maxwell Salvatore was right, after all? What if every wrong turn, every failure, could be erased before it happened?

What if he could have lived a normal life, not haunted by every mistake he'd ever made?

Would that really be so bad?

CHAPTER 32

He opened his eyes and saw light.

Still alive. Somehow, none of Maxwell's zealots had finished them during the night.

He swung his legs off the bed, bracing for the old chorus of creaks and aches. None came. Whatever Andy had said about telomeres and age was true, and working fast.

But that wasn't the only change.

The world felt different. Or maybe it was just him.

Cool floor against bare feet was no longer a shock but a connection—an invisible tether to the vast reserves of energy humming beneath the surface. Awareness pressed in from every direction: the weight of a hundred billion souls who had lived and died, their imprint filling an endless ocean, all of it somehow focused on him.

He was no longer separate from everything that had come before. He was them, and they were him.

The paradox that once mocked him—a world both real and unreal, permanent and fleeting—no longer frightened him. It merely was.

He dressed and ambled to the kitchen. Sunlight filtered through the window and onto his skin, photons spilling from a star born of others long dead, a chain of endings and beginnings that had birthed rock, then water, then life. Would other beings someday look up and discover the same truth? Would they choose to nurture and respect it—or, like humanity, come close to wasting the gift?

A soft tap interrupted his thoughts. "Good morning."

Andy yawned as he fumbled with a stovetop coffee pot. The coffee tin, still sealed, suggested the apartment had been unused for some time. They stood in silence until the little pot gurgled to life, and he poured steaming coffee into heavy ceramic mugs.

"You never said how it went with Evangeline?"

He shook his head. "Not good."

"Tell me."

He shook his head again. "I wanted to tell her... everything. And I couldn't."

"This must be hard for you. And for her."

A sad chuckle escaped him. "That she's fine with. I forgot I'd sent her a suicide note."

"Ouch."

"Of course, you screwed that all up," he said with a lopsided smile.

She put a hand on his arm. "This is the right thing."

"How do you know this?"

Andy took a sip, watching him over the cup. "I don't have your skills, Prospero. But I knew you couldn't leave."

"I'd ask how, but I think I already know the answer."

She shrugged in response. "Despite Maxwell's best efforts, free will still exists. And with it comes uncertainty."

They sipped in silence for a few minutes.

"I've been dreaming about my daughter."

Andy placed her cup down. "Tell me."

He shook his head. "She was alive. We were together, Jeanine and I. Our adopted children grew up normal."

Andy studied him, as if waiting for more.

"It was very real. Like it had really happened. But I knew it was a dream. And Evangeline wasn't there."

Her jawline rippled, and she took another sip. He opened his mouth to continue, but a sudden knock at the door halted his words. He tapped on the kitchen tablet and saw Nora and Miles standing outside.

She walked in first, setting a brown bag on the counter. Dalton handed out scones and cups of strong, sweet coffee.

"So, what is next today?"

His stomach fell as Miles and Dalton exchanged an uneasy glance.

"Evangeline See is missing."

His world stopped. "What do you mean, missing?"

"Our liaison never made it to the hotel with her."

"That's not...she can't just vanish. Did she go somewhere else?"

"We don't know that."

"You lost her?" Prospero barked. "You had one job—"

"Mister Jones, please listen to me—"

"She's alive," Prospero cut in. "I know it. If you don't know where she is...

"She may have left on her own, Mister Jones." Dalton exchanged a wide-eyed glance at Nora Brooks. "She may have decided not to take Tampa up on the offer and decided to go elsewhere. We just can't find her."

He slumped onto the small apartment sofa and buried his head in his hands. "Oh my god, he took her."

"Mister Jones, we cannot assume—"

"HE TOOK HER!"

Mist blossomed into the air as the apartment's heat coiled in him, crawling like thunder. What good were these idiots if they couldn't even protect the one person who—

"Prospero, please," Andy said, cutting through the fog.

Dalton's handgun was out now, aiming at his eyes.

Then a voice, sharp and intimate, sliced through him.

This is your fault

She is lost because of you.

Maxwell. The voice he would never forget. The cruelty that had launched him from a tower now pressed into his mind, a vise squeezing sanity away. His chest tightened as Evangeline's face swam just out of reach...

Then more, this time the roar of a billion voices.

Do not follow him

An ocean of minds, older and deeper, whispering in languages he could understand yet not name, submerged his panic until only clarity remained.

You are not him

He slowed his breathing, his heartbeat, as his mind came alive with a chorus.

You will find her

The mist cooled around him as energy melted from his hands. He sat back, releasing his hold on everything. Lights flickered back on, and the microwave beeped with relief.

"Are you the one?"

Nora Brooks had gone still. She clasped her hands, eyes wide, lips moving as if in prayer. Her eyes flicked to Prospero's. For an instant, he saw it — wide, unguarded, belief, terrifying in its honesty. Then she glanced at her partner, and the professional mask snapped back into place.

Dalton lowered his weapon and stared, slack-jawed. "What the hell was THAT?"

He was searching for an answer when someone knocked on the door.

"Pete, please open up. I have a message for you."

Jeanine's voice. His ex-wife sounded terrified.

CHAPTER 33

Miles kept his weapon low, checking the door camera before stepping toward the entrance.

"You're not going to shoot my ex-wife, are you?" Prospero whispered.

"Maybe after I shoot you," Dalton hissed in his ear, before taking his spot. "Open slowly."

Jeanine—accompanied by Liam, the scumbag who'd slept with her while they were still married—stood in a shaft of early sunshine. She glanced at Andy and raised an accusatory eyebrow.

"Did you get tired of Eve and her microscopic trousers?"

At any other time, Prospero would've taken the bait. His ex-wife, incapable of kindness, only knew to communicate by hurting. Deep down he understood why: the death of Tabitha had taken her soul and destroyed whatever faith she had left in humanity. She'd hated life, the world, and herself, pursuing affairs to justify her self-esteem when her husband, too distraught by dealing with his pain, could not build up hers.

How did he know this? Perhaps this was not the first time this tragedy had struck a human soul. It would not be the last.

For an instant he considered responding with kindness. Cruelty would not do in this situation, and honesty had kept its value since the dawn of humanity.

So he smiled. "I don't think I'll ever tire of Eve's clothing. Andy is my friend."

Jeanine stiffened at the unexpected retort. Prospero gestured them in, and Nora closed the door behind them.

"And these are my newest friends, Miles and Nora. They're armed and trained, so I wouldn't make any sudden moves if I were you. Folks, this is Jeanine, my ex-wife. And Liam, her college flame, and next former husband, the guy with whom she cheated on me."

Liam stiffened at the jab, but remained silent when he noticed Nora's firearm by her side.

Jeanine's jaw rippled with something like restraint. "Your manners have not improved, Pete. We're here to deliver something." She reached into her purse, stopping when Miles barked for her to stop. Andy took the purse, pulling out a lilac envelope. Her face turned ashen.

Jeanine gave a curt, mechanical nod. "We wish you all a wonderful day. Liam and I will be leaving now. Heading for an all-day cruise."

Her face turned away first. Liam stood for an instant, grounded to the spot, then tapped his glasses and followed Jeanine into the morning sun.

"That was the height of..." Prospero trailed off. Andy held the lilac envelope in a shaking hand.

"Are you okay?"

"This is from Maxwell."

"How do you know?"

Andy dropped the card on the table. "Because I gifted him these notecards. In 1930."

She looked away as he opened the card. Nora and Miles holstered their weapons and watched.

Prospero,

You call me a villain because I would end free will.

You're mistaken.

I know you. The failures. The daughter who never had a chance. The stepchildren you never met, now raised by a man you hate. The late nights begging the past to change, because you made the wrong choices—again and again. You cling to free will as if it grants you meaning. But what has it given you, Prospero? What has choice ever delivered but suffering?

Didn't it drive you to end your own life?

Choice is a sickness. An evolutionary flaw. We treat it like power, when it's merely noise, an illusion we're told to worship. But in truth, it only paralyzes us with regret and ruin. The world offers no kindness, and still we insist on choosing our way to destruction.

Our species fails, again and again. Left to our own devices, we always make the wrong choices, placing us on a path to extinction.

Look up into the night. Do you see any signs

of sentience in the sky? Any messages from our galactic siblings? You don't, because they destroyed themselves. Free will ensured it. At some point, every advanced civilization chooses extinction.

I will not allow that to happen.

I will save us—from ourselves. From the illusion of control. From the seduction of agency. I have already begun: draining attention, ambition, decision. I've seeded the belief that outcomes are inevitable. And now, as people stop deciding, they can simply exist. They'll live knowing tomorrow is certain. That's the gift, Prospero. That's true freedom.

And I can give it to you.

No more fear. No more doubt. No more what-ifs.

You hate me because deep down you want what I offer. You recoil from me because I remind you of the part of yourself you've buried. You want to believe that choice defines your humanity. But you know better. You know what choice cost you. Her name was Tabitha.

I offer release—from pain, from consequence, from hope.

You and I share a gift. We are not bound by human limits. We can change the world. Together, we could steer ten billion minds toward unity, not chaos. Toward certainty, not regret. I've already taken the first step. Join me.

Evangeline is with me. She resists—for now. But she will understand. They all do. Freedom is a cancer. I offer Fate as the cure.

This is not a threat, Prospero. This is the last choice you ever need to make—the one that will set you free.

My door is open.

Maxwell

CHAPTER 34

The lilac paper trembled in his hands, its weight greater from the message carried. Maxwell's words coiled around Prospero's mind, burrowing into corners dark with regret.

The letter slipped from his grip and floated to the floor when he collapsed on the chair. Andy stared at it, lips curled in fear.

He stared at the wall as a hollow ringing filled the room. Every choice—every turn he had taken—had led him to this moment. And what had it amounted to? A lifetime of failure. A marriage that had rotted away. A career that floundered. A woman who was everything, now in the hands of a man who thought free will was a disease.

I have nothing left.

Rage swelled from deep inside, sharp and bitter. It wasn't just Maxwell. It wasn't just this twisted, impossible reality into which he'd been thrown. It was everything—the inexorable march of time, the inescapable trap of fate. Hadn't everything been set into motion long before he even knew what he wanted? Was he always going to end up here, a failed man chasing ghosts of what could have been? Destined to make the wrong choice, again, and again, and again, and—

"Prospero?"

He snapped.

"What do you want, Andy?"

"I just wanted you to—"

"Pretend this is all fine? Pretend I still have a choice? You keep telling me to move forward, but move forward into what? Another failure? Another mistake?" He buried his face in his hands. "I have done nothing but *choose*, and every damn choice has been *wrong*!"

She took a breath, but he didn't let her speak. His voice rose now, large and chipped at the edges, blasting the silence.

"I lost my wife, Andy! I lost my daughter. My life. My wife adopted two kids I never met to spite me. And now Evangeline is—" His throat closed around the words. "She's gone."

"She's not gone. There is still hope."

"THERE IS NO FUCKING HOPE!"

The roar blasted from him, heat and light and the end of the world.

And then, darkness.

A BREEZE SWEPT through the open back porch, warm and familiar. The scent of forest, cut grass, and spring. At the far end of the yard, a hedge of trees. Beyond it, the park where he'd walked with Jeanine as her belly grew with life.

A space that had once been home.

Prospero blinked. He *was* home. Their first home — the one they bought on hope and sacrifice, expecting something far different from what fate provided.

He shook his head to wake up. Dreaming of Tabitha was one thing. This memory—the days before her death—seemed unnecessarily cruel.

He shook again, managing only a faint shadow of disorientation. Everything in this dream seemed too... real.

The living room jutted from the home exactly as he remembered—an addition to the study, little more than an afterthought. Sunlight filtered through paper blinds, spilling onto the old futon couch neither of them could give up. The shelf that would never be filled with a dead daughter's scrapbooks. This dream took place before she—

A book lay on the armrest. His chest tightened.

Then, a sparkle of laughter.

A little girl—golden-haired, beaming—bounded toward him in a pink jumpsuit.

He froze and felt his heart stop.

Tabitha.

She was seven, maybe eight. He'd never seen this face, but knew it was his daughter. Alive. Smiling. *Here.*

"Daddy, would you read to me?" She held out the book, her tiny hands gripping the treasured possession.

He took the book, touching her tiny hands, feeling the jolt of life as he held onto the dream. Tabitha bobbed with pent-up energy, giggles leaking from a smile brighter than any sun. He sank onto the couch, hands shaking, wondering if he would dare touch her. His pulse pounded as his mind screamed, *this is a dream.*

Then she snuggled her perfect warmth into him, as if gifting her honeysuckle scent was the most normal thing in all the worlds. He kissed her head, barely containing a sob, even in the dream.

"Read it, Daddy!"

He smiled and read Rudyard Kipling's "How the Camel Got His Hump," somehow knowing all the beats, as if he could map Tabitha's laughter to the words.

I never read this to her. She never lived.

"Are you okay, Daddy?"

"I am, sweetheart," he said, feeling hot tears dampen her hair. "I am."

"What happens when we die, Daddy?

He stopped mid-breath. "What did you say?"

Did she know? He turned to her and met her bright gaze. Clear, honeyed eyes, like her mother's.

Tabitha shrugged. "I just wonder what happens if dying is like falling asleep. Would I ever know?"

He tried to speak, and the book fell from his grasp.

"Why do you ask me that?"

She shrugged again, delighting in the curiosity. "I just wonder. I think about a lot of things."

She slipped off the couch, chasing another sunbeam. A mote of dust hung in the air, stopping the world. He shut his eyes, focusing on the shadow of warmth left by her presence, willing himself not to lose it. If this was a dream, perhaps he did not wish to wake up. But after a few moments he opened his eyes, thankful Tabitha had not seen him crumble.

How accurate was this phantom?

He walked to the stairs, mapping the home with every memory of the tragedy that broke them.

"Jeanine?" he whispered.

She took the stairs up from the basement, her face knit in confusion. Jeanine—not yet his ex-wife—regarded him with an arched brow. "You okay?"

"Where are..."

"What?"

He held on to the iron railing to the basement den, trying not to faint. The cool metal seemed in dire need of paint.

"Nothing. I, ah..."

His mind struggled to process the experience. This was no dream: too accurate, too many sensations, too real. Beneath Jeanine's gaze—augmentation-free, in this dream—he saw it: that old love, mixed with something dark. Jeanine had loved him — *did* love him, in this dream—as certainly as he loved her. The unplanned pregnancy that brought them together had a name, and with it, a commitment. In this life, Tabitha kept them together, although they should have walked their own paths long ago.

But Tabitha had died, stillborn at eight months. Her death had destroyed Jeanine, leading them to try again. Adopted twins were the cruel antidote to the stepsister they never knew, the siblings who never came.

Twins adopted by parents desperate to return from the damned, destined to fill a chasm impossible to close, then forgotten by a woman consumed by grief and guilt.

He walked in a haze the rest of the afternoon, remaining in this new world long past when he thought the dream might end. Dinner was not a family affair. Jeanine set out a plate for him and Tabitha, ordered out, then disappeared downstairs with her wine, where Prospero swore he could hear the sharp inhalations of desperate tears.

That night he slept next to a stranger. Jeanine's body, younger and less manipulated than her other self, felt alien, untouchable, and cold. He rolled over — he always slept on the right side of their bed—and cried himself to sleep.

CHAPTER 35

For a golden moment, before he opened his eyes, he imagined the cruelty of the dream had passed.

It hadn't. He woke up in a cold bed, Jeanine already dressed and preparing for the day. Tabitha, too real in her vibrancy, prepared for school with unrestrained glee. Despite her energy, the rituals of family life felt hollow, as if a thin sheet had been laid on reality, ready to break at the most unexpected moment. When Jeanine lied about running errands after dropping off Tabitha, he waved goodbye in relief.

But saying goodbye to his daughter, even for only part of the day, crushed his soul. He waved at them, closed the door behind him, and broke down.

Only one person could help make sense of this. He was far away in Massachusetts in this new world, half a continent away from Florida. But if he could just talk to Evangeline, perhaps everything would fall into place.

He gazed at the backyard, resplendent in the cool spring morning. Evangeline would've loved the emerald green surrounding everything, her aquamarine eyes lighting up in the dappled sunlight. Thinking about her smile, her voice, and her warmth made the morning tolerable.

His heart hammered as he noticed "his" phone. It wasn't the ubiquitous Apex handset he saw in every hand back "home," the tool he now understood to be Maxwell Salvatore's weapon. On the back gleamed a metallic, stylized version of the logo for Macintosh Computers, a company long ago shuttered. The screen flickered to life—recognizing his face—and he noticed the world was... wrong. Yahoo was little more than a site aggregator. Its place, a company that had misspelled the word "googol" was the go-to navigation of the 'net. The phone opened up a Safari browser, something that had gone extinct decades past. No Firefox, no MyLife, no PicTalk. In their place, strange names: Chrome, Facebook, Instagram. He fumbled his way through this alien digital world in search of Evangeline, desperate for something that made sense.

He first searched for Sirius Java, the center of his life in Mullet Cove. After several minutes of searching, he went cold. Mullet Cove did not exist in this world. In its place, a town called Tarpon Springs, a palimpsest of his home. The googol site allowed for street-level views, which broke his heart. In the space that Sirius Java had occupied stood a converted cafe named Urban Grounds. He paged through their online posts in desperation.

In this world, Angie was Annie: still owned the shop, but hadn't married that idiot George.

And there was no sign of Evangeline See.

He pored over every page on the coffee shop site. Evangeline, or whoever she'd be in this world, had never set foot there.

He grew desperate, finding no sign of her. Was this new

world so cruel, so forlorn, that Evangeline had never been born?

He yanked open the back door, desperate for air and freedom. He crawled through the hedge in the backyard, bursting into the little park where they'd walked their first dog. Emerging from the thicket, he closed his eyes and took a deep breath—hoping, willing, pleading for the act to send him home from this fractured dreamscape.

But nothing happened.

He spent the rest of the day learning about this new world, hating a remote job he could somehow do by rote. The day finished with another silent dinner with a stranger and a daughter that might exist only in his dreams. Night crept upon them with Jeanine lying beside him, a thousand miles away, crying herself to sleep.

The weight of an entire life pressed on him. Here, his daughter lived, but misery still ruled: Evangeline had never met him, or perhaps did not exist. His choice had not led to greater joy or less pain, only a different emptiness.

Was this better?

He'd made different choices, and still carried misery like a cross, with nothing to connect with, no one to help him make sense.

Except perhaps for one other person.

He went back to his phone. Perhaps in this world, she went by another name.

He'd soon find Andromeda Vestal, and discover the truth.

CHAPTER 36

"Sir, are you having trouble?"

"No," Prospero lied, then closed his eyes. "Yes. Yes, I am."

"Just tap on that button," the woman standing by the elevator said, pointing at the icon of an unknown program on his macintosh handset. "They'll pick you up downstairs. First level, last door. Number 107."

"Ah. Of course. You are too kind, madam."

The elevator opened, but the woman stayed, staring at him with a curious smile. "Where's that accent from?"

"I'm from up north," he lied. "Massachusetts. Used to live here in... Tampa."

"I'm from Mass," she said, stopping his breath. "That accent is not one of ours. You must be from the Midwest or something."

"Lived in many places," he said with a nod, and ran off before she found out the truth. He did not glance back as he leapt onto the airport's moving staircase to find his ride to Tarpon Springs.

It was too easy to lie in this world, something that

should've bothered him far more. He felt like used carbon paper, when too many imprints jumble what is left behind. But the vicarious skills that remained in this dream had proven useful in accomplishing the necessary and the mundane.

He'd found Andy after all, except that was not her name. In this world, she'd somehow swapped roles with Evangeline, working at the same coffee shop as Sirius Java. He booked flights the next day, telling Jeanine that he had an urgent out-and back to Tampa, but that he'd be back by midnight. She responded with a shrug, a bellwether of the friction that led to the end of their marriage in his original life.

Perhaps in this world, Prospero had already overstayed his welcome, and Andy Vestal was his only chance. She would have the answers, even if he did not know the questions.

He sat back as the rideshare wended its way north. Every moment highlighted the differences between this world and his. The first indication of something wrong was the heat — far beyond anything he'd experienced in "his" Florida. The air itself seemed to boil, the temperature so oppressive it seemed a physical presence. He tried for a moment to harness its energy, discovering with some alarm that whatever gifts he had back home had not followed him here. The awareness was bittersweet. In a short time he'd grown accustomed to the ability, and losing it felt sufficient penance to see his daughter.

Whatever shadow of himself remained in this dreamworld —if it *was* a dreamworld, and not something he did not wish to accept—he knew some of the basic motions, like finding transportation and purchasing airfare. Something in the recesses of his mind wondered if he'd forget to live in his old world, or if this experience would scar him once he woke up.

But after two days, he'd become convinced this was not a dream.

What it *could* be he was afraid to find out.

He ached for the wonder of Evangeline's smile. But any desire to "go back" evanesced whenever he glanced at his daughter, perfect, vibrant, and alive. This morning, after kissing her in the predawn darkness, he'd almost canceled the trip to Florida, fearful of missing even a few minutes of the dream.

The air boiled as they drove over a long causeway, as if Florida had chosen to burn itself alive. Endless trucks clogged the road. Once back on land, storefronts dotted expansive parking lots devoid of grass or nature, as if built for cars, not people. This world had cut its trees, poisoned its air, then wondered what went wrong.

Maxwell's words screamed into his mind.

Left to their own devices, they always make the wrong choices and end up on the path to extinction.

He closed his eyes, contemplating finality across worlds, as they drove on.

Tarpon Springs welcomed him, an oasis from the heat. The streets seemed familiar, as if someone had taken an image of Mullet Cove and rebuilt it from a fractured memory. The town had not escaped the region's unexplainable zeal to destroy every source of shade, but stood apart from the rest, enjoying the comfort of standing trees and narrow streets. He strolled the main drag — fewer apartments on second floors, more cars, less green — amusing himself by highlighting differences.

This world's Sirius Java—Urban Grounds—occupied the same corner of his familiar world. But other changes puzzled him. Bobby's bar had transformed into a bistro.

Johnny's was now a brewery, swapping places with a squat building sprouting from a parking lot, and the pizza place had switched locations with a tiny museum on opposite ends of the street. He imagined looking at his home through a kaleidoscope: every color present, except somewhere else.

He walked into the coffee shop, holding the familiar door to keep from fainting. The pastry counter and the coffee station were in their proper place, but someone had converted the upstairs into a delightful mezzanine instead of the storage space from Mullet Cove. He stepped to the counter to order and caught his breath.

"How may I help you?"

He tried to speak, but couldn't. This world's Andy was younger—maybe forty?—muscular, and lean. Her short hair was brown, not flecked with gray, and her eyes toyed between amber and something dark.

"Andy? Is this you?"

"I'm sorry?"

"Are you... Andy? Andy Vestal?"

She smiled, but her eyes didn't. "I'm sorry, no. What can I get you?"

He could not stop staring at Andy, or whoever she was.

"A... a black coffee, please."

"Americano?"

Not knowing what she meant, he nodded.

"Anything else?"

"Do you know anyone named..."

He swallowed and turned to find a small queue behind him.

"Never mind," he murmured, and fumbled with his phone to pay the bill. A sense of profound dread engulfed him. He'd traveled for hours to find his last hope, only to meet a stranger.

Andy's twin, or whoever she was, set her jaw and stared at him. "Name?"

"It's... Pete."

"I'll call you when it's ready, Pete."

He almost bumped his head on the stairs up to the mezzanine. Back home, Angie had installed a fire escape ladder, a never-ending source of comments from the patrons. He looked up at couples deep in conversation and felt something hot come over him.

In this world, Maxwell Salvatore did not exist. He had not conspired to snatch attention from the world. Outside, a mad, hot, and harried world confirmed Maxwell's warnings of self-destruction. He stared at the patrons, deep in conversation, and his eyes prickled with hot tears.

He stared at the video screen—in this world far smaller than in his—playing strange reels, which he understood to be animated fare for children. The background music reminded him of a foreign country's attempt at dubbing audio in another language. This he expected: the musicians and artists and filmmakers of *his* world did not exist *here*.

Perhaps, neither did Andy.

The woman who looked like her poured a shot of rich coffee into a paper cup, filled the rest with hot water, then closed the lid, all while staring at him.

"Americano for Pete? Was that to go?"

He nodded before he caught her eye. "Yes. Please."

She placed the drink on the counter and furrowed her eyes. "Are you okay?"

Prospero shook his head. "I'm looking for a friend. You look just like her."

She stared at the wood and raised her eyebrows with a thin smile.

"This isn't some attempt at flirting. I swear. I... you... you look just like her. Like you could be her..."

"Her daughter?" His nod of admission defused the discomfort. "Where is she from?"

He wanted to ask her the same—where was her accent from?—and realized he was the alien in this world.

"I... I don't know. But I need to find her."

"Tried her social media?"

"I did, but I'm not sure I know how."

She tilted her head, and her lips curled into a smile.

"I swear. I'm not very familiar with... social media."

She opened her palm, and it took him a moment to realize she was asking for his handset.

He handed it over, and she handed it back almost immediately. "You have to unlock it."

"Ah, yes."

She motioned to another barista and moved to the side while she tapped away on the screen. After a few moments, she smiled with a silent chuckle.

"You weren't lying about the mother-daughter thing. Is this her?" She showed him the screen, and his heart raced.

"Yes, my god, how did you—"

"Not many people have the name Andromeda. Should've told me that first."

"We, ah, both use different names."

"What's yours?"

"My real name is Prospero," he said, smiling for no reason.

"Cool. Parents into Shakespeare?"

"Who?"

"C'mon. *The Tempest? 'This thing of darkness I acknowledge mine'?*"

"You mean, Marlowe?"

"That's funny. I loved that movie." She raised an eyebrow and tilted her head. "The bad news about your friend Andromeda is that she lives far away."

His heart sank. He could swim in this strange ocean, but in neither world was he made of money. "Where?"

"Says here she's in a little town in Connecticut, over the border from Springfield, Massachusetts. I'm sure you could find her address."

He shut his eyes before the tears burst.

"Are you okay?"

"I am," he replied. "I don't know how to thank you."

"It's okay. You're welcome, Prospero," she replied. "Enjoy your coffee."

He turned to leave, remembering so many times when Evangeline had said the same thing, and stopped.

"Yes?"

"Would you... help me find someone else?"

CHAPTER 37

The woman who was not Andy had a kind heart, taking far more time to help him than he could've ever expected.

It took her a full two minutes to find Evangeline. Out of morbid curiosity, she appended "nee" before her last name. When she showed him her image, his heart broke.

Evangeline Vandemere (nee See) worked on the technical team of BP, which in this world focused on massive oil platforms in the Gulf of Mexico. She had finished her PhD and had never worked at the coffee shop. Her blue-green eyes looked deep-set and dark in the official-looking photo. Her smile—the brightness that lit up his world—was gone, replaced by something tired, fake, and banal. She must've been younger in this world, but she'd aged in ways he could not imagine. This world had provided riches to Evangeline See and taken her soul. Did she also suspect this was not her world?

"Are you okay?" the woman who was not Andy asked.

He nodded. "I, uh, I knew her. Before she..." The words caught deep in his chest. "Before she married."

"Yeah. Everyone wonders what life might have been like if they had made different decisions."

"I'm living through that now."

"Well, Prospero, wherever you are, the best you can do is the best you can do."

"That's very wise."

"I think I saw that on a T-shirt." She shrugged and smiled. "When do you return home?"

He glanced at his phone. "Few more hours before I have to go to the airport."

"You're welcome to stay here. And there's a bookstore on the back side of the block."

He raised his paper cup in thanks and stepped outside into the hellish sun. Half a block was enough punishment in this world, but the bookshop's green awning offered precious shade, an invitation to slow down and think. He stepped inside to the cool scent of books and peace, as familiar as anything this world could offer.

Shelves stocked with alien books covered the walls. Each title—different from back home, yet somehow recognizable—provided a map to overlay this world onto his. The science section was small, but well-stocked. Out of curiosity, he opened a book on quantum science, hoping to find more clues to this reality. Everything he read suggested the rules of the cosmos appeared constant, yet provided no inkling on how to return. But after a few minutes of reading, curiosity turned to despair. In this world, Eugene Wigner's work had been met with skepticism and scorn. No sign existed of Devdan Kinzer, Wigner's protégé. This was a stark reality, where wonder seemed destined for obscurity. No wonder that in this life, Evangeline had lost her soul.

He closed the book before he ruined it with his tears.

"Are you okay?" The proprietor, a young woman with dark hair and kind eyes, surprised him with a whisper.

He nodded, wiping his face. "Sorry. I just found out... I've lost someone."

"I'm so sorry. Here." She looked like the lead singer of a rock band, yet somehow produced a tissue out of nowhere.

"Thank you," he said, wiping his eyes. "By the way, have you heard of *The Tempest*?"

"Shakespeare is in the classics." She picked up a handful of books and motioned with a nod. "Over here."

That had been only a few hours ago, before boarding the flight to Boston. By the time his flight landed, the weight of Evangeline's loss had crushed him. He spent the long drive home thinking of her, lost and adrift in the same world.

He labored up the steps to their home, heavy with regret. The icy reception from a soon-to-be-estranged wife cemented the feeling of malaise, a liminal dislocation he seemed powerless to escape.

Dinner felt like a pantomime. Jeanine set down plates, Tabitha chattered about school, and still Prospero felt like an intruder, a ghost at his own table. His daughter lived, but his marriage was already ashes, the gulf between them wide as despair.

He lay awake long after Tabitha went to bed, long after Jeanine's fractured sighs gave way to restless sleep. He rolled over to check the address on his handset. Andy Vestal—the real one, he hoped—lived only two hours away.

The next morning, he kissed Tabitha goodbye. Her laughter pierced the bright kitchen, gifting it with perfection. Jeanine seemed almost relieved when he told her he'd be gone for several hours.

The drive south felt like a game. Cars he'd never seen,

fueling stations he could not imagine, towns the wrong size and in the wrong place. Something called "Dunkin Donuts" seemed to sprout from every clutch of buildings like pink mold. Different choices were made in this world; some good; others catastrophic.

Like his life: a daughter who lived, a wife who grew more distant every day. A monotonous job, devoid of satisfaction.

And worst of all, Evangeline's brilliance turned into despair.

Perhaps free will was merely the courage to keep choosing when every choice hurt; an unending path of regret where pain offered the only reward.

He arrived at an apartment complex erupting with fresh flowers, an enthusiastic acknowledgment of the end of another New England winter. He nodded with nervous energy as the desk attendant looked up the room.

"Upstairs, left at the landing. Room 273."

He leapt up the airy staircase, for a moment suspended in time, and paused before knocking on the door.

This is my choice. A moment that only I own, which may define everything that follows.

He rapped on the door, heart in his throat.

"Who is it?"

"My name is Prospero Jones. I'm looking for someone named Andromeda Vestal."

Silence. Then a shuffling, the unlocking of latches, and Andy Vestal opened the door.

In this world, something had changed. She was older than expected, yet somehow at peace. For an instant, Prospero thought, *not again.*

Then she broke into a soft smile and touched his face. Her hands were warm, suffused with something like hope.

"You always find me," she whispered. "No matter what world."

CHAPTER 38

Andy held his hand and ushered him in. Her apartment felt spartan, as if a prisoner had decided to enjoy their sentence, and embarked on making confinement their home. Behind angular furniture, a glass door opened up to views of a bright green forest. Sensible decor, providing just enough comfort, seemed chosen to calm the mind. No figurines or kitsch anywhere—only the prosaic necessities for a long and mindful life.

"How are you?" She whispered, as if allowing him to take in the scene.

"I still don't know if this is a dream."

"It isn't. Are we fighting him?"

The comment startled him. "How do you know?"

"Sit down. Tea?"

He nodded and stared outside as she set the kettle and cups. The second-floor apartment gifted them expansive sight lines over green hills. Far beyond, the shimmer of towns. Beyond that, the horizon.

All of it a new world, forged by different decisions.

She set the mug on a wooden coffee table adorned with a miniature cactus and three framed photos: a picture of a young boy, and two pictures of young families. One was old, familiar.

"In this lifetime, Maxwell and I have a son."

He picked up the photograph. A younger Andy held a baby in her arms. Maxwell Salvatore, this time beaming with a kind smile, embraced her from behind. The sepia-toned image must've been taken decades ago.

"Is this him?" He picked up the other photograph.

"Massimo died when David was young. He loved him and never saw him grow up." She gazed at the photo, tracing a finger over the glass.

"Was Maxwell trying to enslave humanity in this world, too?"

"No. Others seem to have gravitated toward that obsession." She shook her head with a sad smile. "In this world, Massimo was passionate and kind. He passed away from leukemia."

"I'm sorry. I guess." He scratched his scalp, forgetting he had hair in this life. "I'm not sure how to convey condolences in this situation."

"Loss and grief give meaning to both dreams and reality."

"And what about your son?"

"David is an accountant," Andy replied with a proud smile. "I don't think he has plans to enslave humanity, either. He has a beautiful wife and daughter. I am a lucky grandmother."

"So... you're not one hundred years old?"

She chuckled at him. "Not everything works out the same in every timeline."

He raised an eyebrow and nodded, taking a sip of tea.

"Black tea, honey and cream. How did you know?"

"I've known you for ages, Prospero."

"No, Andy. Where I come from, we just met. How do you know me?"

"This you,"—she pointed at him—"Has met me today. Somewhere else, it may be days; somewhere beyond that, perhaps years. We've been friends across space and time."

"The many-worlds interpretation," he muttered. "I thought that was a mathematical trick. It isn't, isn't it?"

She shook her head in reply.

He winced. "That means there is no free will. If every outcome exists, in all possible worlds, I don't choose anything. I'm just aware of whatever universe I end up in."

"Close, but incomplete."

"How? I'm here now, in this crazy universe with pink doughnut shops on every corner."

She took a sip of tea. "Don't bother with those. The coffee is terrible."

They laughed at the joke. He realized it was the first time he'd felt joy since his last night with Evangeline—in another life, another timeline, another world.

"We exist in all of them, Prospero. Every choice you've ever made—every choice you didn't make—created another path, another version of you, another version of me."

He swallowed hard. "So, there's—what? Infinite versions of me? Of you?"

She shrugged. "Not infinite. But vast. Each one branching, shifting, rewriting itself with every decision, no matter how small. In some, you never met me. In others, we found each other lifetimes ago. In some, you never even knew Evangeline. And in some... she's the one standing here instead of me."

The thought made his chest tighten. "And in this world?"

"In this world, you never became who you were supposed to be. Neither did I." She sighed. "Neither did Evangeline. And neither did Maxwell."

"So how can we be having this conversation? If I'm just a nameless nobody in a lousy marriage? In a timeline I didn't want?" The words ripped him as they spilled from his lips.

In this world, Tabitha lived.

She nodded, perhaps sensing the guilt. "When Maxwell and I started our journey, which has happened in every timeline, the world was fascinated by what Bohr and others had discovered. Then came the many-worlds interpretation, which said that what we see is merely what happens in our universe."

She placed her hands together as if in prayer. "Then von Neumann and Wigner changed everything. They understood that consciousness wasn't just an observer—it was a part of the universe itself. And that's when we began to understand."

"I thought those three were always incompatible. And we chose the one that gave the least agency to humanity."

She raised her index finger. "The Copenhagen Interpretation explains the world you see. The practical reality. It explains why, when you look at something, it has a definite state. It's useful, but it's not the complete picture—it's just how we experience things moment to moment."

Then she raised a second finger. "Many-Worlds is the real structure of the universe. Every time a quantum event happens, the universe doesn't actually 'collapse.' It splits. All possibilities happen. Every choice, every chance encounter, every moment of doubt—you followed one path, but every other one still exists somewhere."

She raised a third finger and bunched them together. "And this is where von Neumann and Wigner demonstrated genius and wisdom. Your consciousness—our consciousness—chooses which of those paths we experience. We're not just passengers on some cosmic machine. We're the ones steering. We have agency. You could have been someone else, somewhere else, living a different version of your life. But you're here. Because this is the one you're seeing."

Prospero stared at her. "So... consciousness doesn't just collapse reality, it *selects it?*"

Andy nodded. "Like tuning a radio. Every frequency is already there. But the one you focus on? That's the one you hear."

He stayed silent for a long moment.

After a few moments, she continued in a whisper. "Maxwell was right about something. Most intelligent civilizations do end up destroying themselves. But it is not because they have free will. It's because they abandon it."

The twist of his brow told her to continue.

"When civilizations remove free will, their timeline collapses. The big changes never split. After a while, they wither, and die. That's when they become extinct."

The idea slammed into him. "All across... the universe?"

"Yes. *All* the universes."

The ringing in his ears ripped through the silence. "Those are the greatest stakes. Ever."

"That's why we have to stop him." It came out as a statement, utterly out of place from Andy's apartment, as if she were an actress reciting a line in a—

"You're not the Andy from this timeline? Are you?"

Her face blossomed into a wry smile. "I am, and I am not. A few of us — a handful over the millennia — have been able to see into the parallel worlds. Imagine déjà vu, but lasting a lifetime."

He tilted his head with a lopsided smile. "That sounds very familiar."

"Of all of them, Prospero, you are the most gifted."

"I still don't understand. Why?"

"Because, Prospero, you are among the flawed. The perfectly flawed."

He closed his eyes and laughed. "I'm starting to believe that."

Andy leaned closer. "And because deep inside, whether you know it or admit it, this was your choice."

He wanted to argue, to tell her she was wrong, that this was not his choice. But the words never came. Instead of recoiling, he took their weight.

"It doesn't matter what could have been. It never did. The only timeline that matters—the only one that's real—is the one you choose to live in."

He took a deep breath, and stared her in the eye. "So how do I get back? How do I make this right?"

"Let your consciousness be your guide. And Prospero?"

"Yes?"

"Please believe. And don't let that bastard get away with it."

CHAPTER 39

The sunset's rays slanted through the afternoon, bathing the road in a golden glow. The landscape unfurled ahead of him, becoming more familiar with every passing moment. Even the air smelled comforting—that mix of relief at the end of labor, the anticipation of evening, the coming comfort of sleep.

All of that evaporated as he gripped the steering wheel, the weight of his future settling into his chest.

Minutes ago he'd left Andy, lingering at the door in silence, wondering if this was all a dream, or the most important action he would ever take. He stopped and asked her the question burning down his soul.

"Is this going to work?"

She smiled and placed a hand on his cheek. "It has to."

He didn't ask what she meant.

Now, as the car rumbled over ribbons of pavement, he avoided contemplating the path ahead. The light here was softer, the trees brighter, the sky a slight tint darker. But the ache inside him—the familiar pull of loss and longing—was the same. Perhaps Andy was right about being one of the few whose minds transcended time and space.

He pulled into the driveway—his driveway—as the sun settled behind the woods. Shadows stretched across the world. The gloaming, he'd once heard it called. The name seemed perfect. He sat in the car for a moment, steeling himself for the second most difficult night of his life. He had never been here before—coming home late to his daughter and his distanced wife—and yet, he had. The home he had shared with Jeanine, the life they'd once tried to build—here it stood, undisturbed by choice or fate.

In another life, everything had turned out differently.

He took a deep breath and walked the stone steps up to the door. For an instant, he swayed. Did he see a shimmer in this dreamscape? Was the scent of new grass and springtime real?

For now, in this world, it was. As real as anything.

Inside, small peals of laughter floated through the house. Tabitha's giggles, small and soft, impossibly perfect, the most beautiful sound he'd ever heard.

They had not existed in his past life.

Would it kill him to make the choice to stay here?

Would he choose a life with his daughter over the end of everything?

She sat cross-legged on the couch, a book nestled in her lap. Her copper curls spilled from behind her ear as she turned a page, a beauty that cracked his soul. Jeanine sat beside her, one arm draped over the back of the couch, her own book in hand. She noticed Prospero and smiled over her reading glasses. This was one of the good days, he remembered from Jeanine's gaze. A scene so normal, so perfect, so lost. He swallowed back emotion before anyone noticed.

Tabitha looked up and beamed. "Hi Daddy! Will you come and read with us?"

His legs carried him forward before he could think. He lowered himself onto the couch, Tabitha nestled between her parents, and he fought the lump in his throat.

"Which one are we reading?"

"The one about the rhinoceros!"

He cleared his throat and read. A few sentences in, she elbowed him.

"Nooo! I want you to say the *par-seee!*" She shook and giggled in delight.

He smiled back a sob, and let it ride. Tabitha hung on every word, biting her lips through laughter as he molded his voice into a story he'd never read aloud. Jeanine curled up her knees and gazed at him with delight.

"But the Par*see* came down from his palm-*tree*, wearing his hat, from which the rays of the sun were reflected in more-than-oriental splendor, packed up his cooking-stove, and went away in the direction of Orotavo, Amygdala, the Upland Meadows of *Anantarivo*, and the Marshes of Sonaput!"

He closed the book. Tabitha cheered, then enveloped him in a hug, gifting him with the most perfect moment of his life.

She was alive.

And he might never see her again.

Jeanine stroked Tabitha's hair and cheeks, adoring her little girl. "It's late, Tabby. Let's put you to bed."

He watched Jeanine comb Tabitha's hair as she stood on a little stool and brushed her teeth, before she slipped into her favorite bunny pajamas. He carried her onto the bed, kissed her forehead, and tucked a curl behind her ear. She curled her fingers around his hand.

"Why are you crying, Daddy?" she asked.

It felt so normal for her to be so observant. He wiped his tears and pressed his lips to the crown of her head. "Because I love you so very much."

A pause. Then, quieter, as if speaking to the universe, daring it to create something, anything more real than this.

"And I will love you forever, across all the universes, no matter what."

The words hung between them, held together by Tabitha's smile. "I love you too, Daddy. Night."

He stayed in her room, watching her until her breathing slowed, her small body rising and falling in perfect rhythm with the universe. A thin beam of soft light hung between them, the last vestige of twilight, until it, too, vanished between one heartbeat and the next.

He wanted to stay there and weep. What if he just stayed? He'd wake up, and she'd be here tomorrow...

He stopped.

In this world, Tabitha *lived*.

Soon, he would be gone, his consciousness slipping back into a world where she had never existed. But here, this Tabitha—this beautiful, perfect child—would live, with a father who loved her.

She would never know what he had lost. And she would never have to.

Because this life—her life—might not be perfect, but it was beautiful.

He bent over for one last kiss, inhaling the caramel scent of her skin. Then, carefully, he stood, and pulled the door closed.

Jeanine stood outside, watching him. The glow from the hallway bathed her in soft blue light.

"You okay?" she asked.

He nodded, wiping a tear. "I am. Lots on my mind."

In his other life, Jeanine could read him like a book. That skill came with years of loving someone, of knowing them so well that even their smallest gestures carried meaning.

She *had* loved him. And he'd loved her. They were intertwined, the roots of trees that grew apart, but shared something deep and unseen.

She smiled and gestured to the kitchen. Without a word, she pulled two wine glasses from the cupboard, then uncapped an enormous bottle of table wine. They clinked glasses, peering behind for a waking child.

"You've been different the past few days. You tucked her in like you'd never see her again."

Her voice had not been this soft for as long as he could remember. He wanted to tell her, to share the impossible with the woman he'd once loved, the mother of his child.

But what could he say?

I don't belong here. I have to go back to a place where we lost ourselves when we lost her, a place where I love someone else.

Because for some reason, I have to save the world.

Because if I don't, I'll forever lose my daughter, the one I will love across all the universes, until the end of time.

I failed us once. I won't fail us again.

He took a slow breath and took a sip. "You know, sometimes you just look at the world, and realize how fragile it all is. How we can lose it. I want to remember while I'm here. In this moment."

He reached out and held her hand.

She smiled in surprise. She was older than the last time he'd seen her. No, that wasn't right. She was exactly as she should be—no augmentations, no carefully constructed mask to hide grief. Just Jeanine. The way she would have been in another world.

"You ever think about how things could have been different?" he asked.

She let out a soft laugh, shaking her head. "All the time."

"What would you have changed?"

Jeanine considered that, tilting her wine glass. "I don't know. Maybe nothing. Maybe everything. But I stopped worrying about 'what ifs' a long time ago."

He swallowed. "Why?"

She shrugged and met his gaze. "Because it doesn't change anything. We are who we are. We just have to make the best decision and move on."

For the first time in a long time, he saw her, and understood. Jeanine's pain had never been just about Tabitha. It was something deeper—something intrinsic to her soul. Perhaps she had always carried that sadness, even before their daughter's death. Perhaps it was part of her, just as regret had always been part of him.

And maybe—just maybe—that was okay. Jeanine had made her decisions. Not all were perfect. But all of them were hers.

He caressed her hand, and she didn't pull away.

"When was the last time I told you I love you?"

She took a halting gasp, then blossomed into a smile. "Do you have any idea how much that means right now?"

He shrugged in response. Words seemed too fragile, too dangerous.

"Pete. Are you trying to seduce me?"

He smiled and said nothing.

Then she took his hand and pulled him towards the bedroom. "Come with me."

CHAPTER 40

Darkness peeled away in waves.

Prospero gasped, sucking in air as if surfacing from deep water. The ceiling above him came into focus: chunks of plaster missing, the charred remains of a blast. The air hung thick with smoke. He took a deeper breath, and coughed.

Andy loomed over him, cradling his head. "You with me?"

He nodded. Everything hurt. Had he fallen asleep?

He sat up and noticed the room. Light slipped through a broken windowpane; dust and debris cluttered the floor. Tables and chairs jumbled against the walls, overturned. Large chunks of sheetrock had blasted open, revealing wooden beams holding up metallic mesh.

Then, panic. He'd been gone for days. Whatever Maxwell had threatened had long ago passed.

Andy crouched beside him, studying him with burning intensity.

"Did you find me?"

He caught his breath in a moment of confusion. "What?"

Then he noticed the gleam in her gaze, and nodded.

Her cheeks flushed, and she bit her lip. "How long?"

"I was there for...three days?"

She unfurled a sly smile, a first for her. "How'd I look?"

He let out a painful chuckle and squeezed her hand. "You look better here."

She winked at the secret. "So, what did you discover?"

He sat up. The weight of it all pressed into him—the ache of loss, the certainty of what had to come next.

"I think... we had to stop him?"

"We have time. You've only been out a minute."

"What?"

She blossomed into a knowing smile. "The universes don't all share the same speed limit."

She helped him to his feet. For a moment the room tumbled, then settled. In the corner behind the breakfast table, Nora and Miles huddled together, unscathed, at the center of a perfect, undamaged circle traced on the wall and floor. Outside the tracing, plaster and sheetrock had atomized into dust.

He had done all of this. But How?

Miles stared open-mouthed, gripping his knees. Nora sat cross-legged, staring at him with wide eyes.

"We're going to be okay, aren't we?" Her tone answered her own question.

Prospero nodded. "I hope so."

"We don't have much time to waste," Andy added.

"I know what I have to do." He stood, taking inventory of his aches, and willed himself to the door. "Can I borrow your car?"

Miles scrambled to his feet. "Our car? You can't leave like

this. You set off a bomb, Mister Jones! You've destroyed a Federal safe house. Now —"

Nora touched his arm. "It's okay. This is now beyond us."

She pulled a set of keys from her jacket and pressed them into Prospero's palm. "Take the car. And please," she whispered, "make it right."

He nodded his thanks and followed Andy out the door.

———

THE PARKING LOT seemed peaceful in the aftermath of whatever he'd caused in the apartment. The midmorning lull was in full swing, the world deep into their workdays. Everything seemed vast. Even if only minutes had passed in this world — something he still could not comprehend — Jeanine and Liam could be anywhere.

Andy squeezed his arm and nodded. Of course.

He closed his eyes, and thought of her. The Jeanine from the last world, the one where plastic surgery and augmentation had not yet hidden the pain beneath.

And he felt her, a stab of pain as she reckoned with manipulation and betrayal. Liam sat in silence next to her. He could taste the terror of what he'd done.

The connection surged. A thread, thin and unbreakable, pulled him.

A parking lot not far from here.

He peeled out of the wooded apartment complex on instinct. At every turn, something tickled his mind. In minutes, a glow. He pulled into the parking lot of a breakfast restaurant chain, aiming for Liam's gaudy car, parked with doors open in the shadow of a lone tree.

Jeanine sat hunched over in the passenger seat, curled almost into herself, shaking with sobs. Minutes, and a lifetime ago, he'd woken up next to her, happy for the first time in their marriage.

In this timeline, his heart broke. The woman he'd once loved had fallen, and far.

Liam stepped out, trying to speak. Prospero raised a hand and knelt beside his ex-wife.

"Now I understand," he murmured.

She gasped in silence. Makeup and mascara left thick wet streaks on skin stretched beyond reason.

"I can't explain any of this, and it is going to sound crazy," he said. "But in another life, Tabitha lives. It is not a dream. It is as real as this life. She lives. You and I are together. We never adopted the twins."

She sucked in a quick gasp and stilled. "How do you know?"

"I'm not sure I could explain it. But you have to believe me. This isn't a dream, or a hallucination. And I think you know."

Her lips trembled as she avoided his gaze. For a moment, he wondered if she'd ever ask.

"Is she happy?"

He held her hand. "She is. She's beautiful. You love her, and read to her every day. You still hate your life, and I hate my job. But the moments we spend together are priceless."

She broke into a grimace and curled again into sobs.

"Her favorite book is by a man named Rudyard Kipling. *How the Rhinoceros Got His Skin*. I make funny faces, and we all laugh. You made that possible."

She clutched his hand, wet with tears, and nodded. "Can I see her?"

He hesitated. He could rewrite everything and tell her it wasn't too late. But that was a lie. Some fates had already been written. Choices had been made, and destiny played its part. He had to let go. And so did Jeanine.

"She is safe in her life. This one was not hers." He swallowed back a dry sob. "In this life—in all lifetimes—our choices decide our fate. You need to weave your world one choice at a time. Come back to yourself. Confront your past. Make the right choice."

Her lips parted, but no words came.

He squeezed her hand. "I loved you once, Jay. I still do. Our lives may no longer be together, but you need to know. I forgive you. For everything."

She stepped out and embraced him. Her body quivered in spasms, alien and comforting. This was not his life. The choice to end their marriage had been his, as much as it had been hers. But beneath the exterior that he'd once despised, he now saw the truth: a woman broken far before a cruel life destroyed her. How could he blame her for trying to escape?

Hadn't he tried the same, by trying to kill himself?

He stood back and turned to Liam.

"If you stay together, you need to understand, too. Before you take care of her, you need to confront whatever is inside you."

Liam's jaw twitched, as if searching for something to say. Finally, he looked away. "How?"

Prospero studied him. "Start off by being honest with yourself. Stop pretending. Then figure it out."

He turned to leave, then stopped. Jeanine's bleary eyes gleamed with something like hope.

"I know who did this to you. I know it wasn't your choice, and I forgive you for that as well. But if you don't mind, I'm going to break into our old house."

She nodded in understanding, and wiped away tears.

Andy waited by the car. He slid into the driver's seat, started the car, and drove away. At the parking lot exit, he glanced back in the rearview mirror one last time. Jeanine watched after them, unmoving.

"One more stop," he said, pulling into traffic. "Then I'm ready."

CHAPTER 41

The drive south on the highway passed in a blur. Office buildings, strip malls, and hospitals all left behind, all unwitting of the stakes that had yet to play out. Once off the tollway, the roads dissolved into tight, small spaces, until they entered one of the many isolated developments dotting the northern reaches of the Tampa Bay estuary.

The large homes, sterile neighborhoods, and antiseptic streets lay in quiet contrast to the center of Mullet Cove. This was where Jeanine had grown distant after their relocation, where their marriage had collapsed in slow, irreversible steps. A house built for a second-chance life that never quite fit.

He hadn't been to this house in years, and hadn't wanted to. He wondered if the twins he'd barely met were even here, or if Jeanine had ever talked about him. From what he'd gathered in their few talks, the two children spent their lives in the care of others, fated to heal a wound that would never close. After only three days in another world, Jeanine's enforced isolation had made him feel closer to Tabitha.

The neighborhood had changed. He didn't recognize some

faces that passed by, the wary nods of strangers who had continued whatever lives had once intersected with his. Some houses had fresh coats of paint; others stood unchanged, frozen in time. He realized with a wave of regret that he'd never seen the twins in this house.

They parked in the short driveway and stepped into the afternoon, a thick Florida heat somehow softer than the blast of the last world. The walkway skirted past grass he hadn't cut enough, up to the door he'd stood in front so many times, waiting for Jeanine to answer, hoping for life to go back to the way it was.

It never did.

He patted himself for keys out of habit, then stopped. He drew a slow breath and expanded his mind. The locks were simple—metal tumblers, a mechanism waiting for motion. He reached out, feeling the faint hum of fields around him. Move the cylinder just so, a pin up, the other down, picking a lock with his mind.

The lock clicked. He turned the doorknob and pushed inside. The world was becoming easier to control.

But some things could never be made whole again, no matter the timeline.

The house smelled of vanilla and lemon. Candles and cleaner, he suspected: staged, impersonal, and artificial. The decor had changed since he'd left. Andy would recoil at the wave of pastels stretching across the walls, punctuated by maudlin wooden plaques, each stamped with cheerful affirmations.

Life, Love, Laughter
Happy by Choice
Family is Everything

Prospero let out a slow breath. No one in this house had ever lived by those words.

He stepped, respectful and deliberate, through a house smaller than he remembered—as if memory had expanded it, and time had shrunk it down to something unremarkable. The living room gleamed, awash in white carpets and forbidding furniture, with shelves full of hollow fictions of a vanished life.

That's when he saw it.

A small urn sitting on the mantel.

The ashes of their child.

In this world, they had never buried their stillborn Tabitha. Jeanine, crippled by guilt, could never leave her, carrying her ashes through every one of their relocations. Tabitha's remains accompanied them from city to city, state to state, a shadow they could never outrun, hanging over every moment of their lives.

He stepped closer to the tiny vessel, so carefully kept. The brushed surface still gleamed, unchanged since the week they lost her. He touched the cool metal and felt his voice tighten.

"I know you're okay now." His voice barely carried in the bright, empty room. "It wasn't able to be your father in this life. But in another timeline, you are happy and joyful, and you light up the world with your smile."

He swallowed hard.

"I'm about to do something, and I may not come back. If I don't, I want you to know this: the three days I spent with you were the happiest of my life. Of any life."

He wished the time in this universe was as malleable as in others. He stayed there, thinking of his beautiful daughter, for a long time.

She was alive. Not here, but somewhere. She had a father —a man who was him, and not him—who cared for her, and read to her, and would love her to the end of his days. That future, that life, was worth fighting for. Even if it no longer belonged to him.

He kissed the tip of his finger and touched the surface of the urn.

"I love you, Tabby. All across the universe, until the end of time. If I don't come back, I'll find you."

He turned, stealing one last look at the urn, and walked out the door.

Outside, Andy stood under the oak tree. The sky stretched wide and bright, an endless expanse of blue. He looked up, savoring the dappled beams of sunlight pressing into his skin, the delicious feeling of being alive.

They stood in silence for a while. No one needed to read the other's mind.

"I have one question, Andy."

"Not sure I can answer any better than you could."

"If I die doing this, if this is the end...will I see her again? In that life?"

A beam of sunlight speckled the grass, the confluence of light beams from a star toying with a living thing, observed by another. This blink in time would never return. But it had created beauty in the consciousness of a tiny part of the universe, a living part of the cosmos that had become aware of itself. It all seemed so vast, so fleeting, so urgent.

Andy lifted her gaze, tilted her head, and answered his question. "You already did."

"See her?"

"No," she whispered. "You already died."

CHAPTER 42

A warm afternoon breeze carried the scent of trees and caressed his skin. Dry leaves rustled a whisper he could almost understand. He tried to continue, but the words caught, snagged on the edges of the moment.

Everything around him was alive. How could this not be real?

"What do you mean? Is... this all a dream?"

Andy tilted her head, a smirk flickering across her lips. "That's the question no one knows. Because the only certain thing about the universe..." She spread her arms wide, gesturing to the sky. "... is that we're experiencing it."

He felt his skin grow cold even in the afternoon heat. "This isn't the time for riddles, Andy. If I'm already gone, then what is this? A dead man's dream?"

She flashed that grin, the one she reserved for unveiling a secret. "I'm pretty damn sure you're alive. Because I am, and I brought you back."

His heartbeat drummed in his temples. "Now would be a great time to tell me more."

"We kind of knew you were the one," she replied with a shrug.

"You and Kinzer?"

This time, her eyes opened up to the world. "All of us. Me, Kinzer. Every person you've seen driving us across town. There are so many of us, Prospero, who have caressed what is beyond. None of us can see or harness what you wield. But we know about it. We believe it; we know it is possible. After a thousand years, you've proven it true."

He tried to egg her on to continue, and decided a slaw-jawed stare was the best option.

"You have the unenviable fortune of being the one person most entangled with the billions of souls who came before."

He took a sharp inhale, realizing he'd held his breath. Around him, the world sharpened into focus as everything began to make sense. Andy must've read it on his face.

"We're not perfect. I almost stopped you before you went into the water. Maybe it was fear or doubt. It doesn't matter. I hesitated, and for a few moments, you drowned. You were dead."

"And then...?"

"And then I brought you back. Gave you CPR on that nasty little beach where all the kayaks put in. Managed to haul you back."

"Did you perform mouth-to-mouth?"

"I didn't enjoy it, if that's what you're asking," she replied with a playful shove.

"How'd you get me home?"

"I do have a lot of friends. And some skill. Although not like yours."

He tilted his head in a nod. "What happened to me?"

She raised her eyebrows with a heavy sigh. "Humans have

been talking about near-death experiences for longer than we've had religion. Ever wondered why?"

He shook his head. "Not until now."

"Because when the body brushes against death, something breaks. The barrier thins. What's inside us blurs with... everything else. For most people, it's a glimpse—of a parent, a child, someone they've lost. "

"But not for me."

She placed a hand on his chest. "You might be the most entangled person who's ever lived. You didn't see one soul. You touched all; the embers of every soul who has ever lived. And when you came back, they came with you."

He placed his hand on hers and gazed back into the eyes of a friend he'd somehow known for several lifetimes.

"You can't break the laws of nature, Prospero. No one can. But you've become something else. Others collapse one outcome at a time. You collapse possibilities. You can change the universe, not at a microscopic level, but at scale. Our human scale."

He let go of her hand. "That roar, every time something came to me..."

"Yes. Billions of souls don't manifest in voices or lost memory. They *are* you. They guide you. It's not impossible. It's just the beginning."

She turned away and crossed her arms. "And unfortunately, we don't have much time. Maxwell's strength grows. Soon, you will no longer be able to turn him away."

The ultimate sacrifice, he thought, and turned to face the house. Inside lay the ashes of a dead daughter he'd love across time, a daughter who still lived in an alternate world, a daughter he could never bring back.

Because he was not a god or a tyrant. He was just a man.

A man somehow connected to everyone who had come before, who had to stop someone who *did* fancy themselves a tyrant, a wannabe deity bent on making a choice so heinous there would be no further choices beyond.

"So I won't see her again. If I die."

She took a step closer and held his hand. "You'll be part of the same ocean. And you'll find your way together."

A faint smile crossed his face. In this universe, he'd lost much, and gained everything. Death would not be an end, but a door.

"What about…"

Andy squeezed his hand. "What do you think?"

He stared at the grass beneath him, and thought of Evangeline: her smile, her voice, her eyes, the impossible ways in which she was the most interesting person he'd ever met, the most beautiful, the most sensual.

"I told her something that I didn't really understand," he whispered. "Now I do."

"Tell me."

"I told her that of all the lifetimes, I was glad to live in hers."

A wide smile blossomed across her face. "I don't think that was by accident, Prospero. I believe that is your answer."

Then he felt her wipe the tear streaking down his cheek.

"You'd give your life for hers?"

"A thousand times over. Even if we've only just met."

She dropped her gaze. "Now you understand why we trust you."

He tilted his head and knitted his brow. "Because I just realized I'd risk my life for someone I love?"

She nodded. "I loved a man once who turned into a

monster. I want to trust another, who may be our only hope. And the only reason I trust you is because of Evangeline."

When she gazed back up, her eyes misted with tears. "Have you ever wondered, Prospero, that in the scale of the universe, love is the one thing that makes no sense, and yet perfect sense?"

He raised an eyebrow, waiting for more.

"Love is the one force that drives us to sacrifice existence for the unknown. And yet it is also the one force, along with its sister, Hope, which cannot be broken."

She placed a hand on his cheek. "Please, Prospero. For the love of humanity. Do not forget her."

He looked into the sky, the fractured blue beyond the lattice of life casting shadows on his skin. The universe was vast, impossible...and he was part of it, the way it became aware of itself, the way it sacrificed itself, for itself. Preserving that treasure made every defense worthy. Saving the life of one very special being had now become the only thing that mattered—for him, and for everyone.

He squeezed his fists tight, savoring an instant that would evanesce. The future—everyone's future—was built one moment at a time.

And his moment had arrived.

He took Andy's hand, smiled, and turned to the car.

"Now I'm ready."

CHAPTER 43

The tower loomed in the heat, glass and steel catching the late afternoon sun. Clouds swept across the vast sky, scattering fractured beams onto the streets below. Prospero stood still, the only one gazing upward. Around him, people moved with heads bowed, absorbed in a multitude of devices and screens. If that numb choreography proved anything, Maxwell Salvatore's plan to destroy free will was already thriving.

And this was where it began.

Last time, awe had held him—the tower rising like a monument to inevitability. He hadn't seen the trap waiting inside. That day, he'd walked in blind.

Today, the trap still waited. This time, he'd walk in willingly, and prepared.

He crossed into the lobby, heat and humidity shedding from him like a dream. Workers drifted over the marble floor with practiced rhythm—either unaware of what approached, or entwined in it. Even in motion, they surrendered their attention, drifting through simulations behind lenses and screens. In another world, Prospero imagined wealth flaunted through opulent gadgets. Here, people paid to give up their minds. The deeper their detachment from reality, the higher their status—or so society had agreed. Except for the enlightened few who refused: Andy, Evangeline, and him.

And the others like Kinzer, the brave souls whose resistance and devotion had been necessary for his presence here tonight.

He entered the elevator, pressed the button, and felt the car begin its ascent. The structure no longer felt like glass and steel. Now it vibrated with restrained energy, atoms held by invisible tension he could feel under his skin. On his last visit, he'd toyed with heat and currents, amazed at his skill. Those feats now seemed small amusements or sleights of hand. Everything around him hummed, pulsing with power waiting to be drawn, harnessed, and focused.

He prayed it would be enough to stop a madman.

A few floors up, his ears popped, then the doors slid open.

And his heart locked in his chest.

Evangeline stood beside the receptionist, her smile a tight grimace. She held her body too still, as though anchoring herself against a storm. Their eyes met, and for a heartbeat, something flickered—something trapped, but unbroken.

"Evangeline! What did he do to you?"

Her lips parted, but her jaw didn't. "Prospero, how great of you to come." The words scraped out of her. "Come. He's waiting."

She turned—he pictured her teeth grinding with the effort—and led him in.

At the far end of the conference room, Maxwell Salvatore —CEO of Apex Industries, richest man alive, and the ageless husband of Andromeda Vestal—waited at the vast table where he'd once unveiled his twisted dream. This was the same office where Prospero had fallen, to what should have been his death.

Maxwell welcomed him with a vicious smile and open arms.

"Prospero! How nice of you to join me. I trust you've considered my offer?"

"I read your offer. You're insane."

Maxwell's smile held. He glanced at Evangeline, and her posture shifted. For the first time since he'd known her, Prospero's stomach curdled at her smile.

"Wouldn't you prefer a world where Tabitha had lived?"

He stepped forward. "That's your angle? Using her like a puppet to deliver your garbage?"

Maxwell stayed silent, but Evangeline didn't.

"Wouldn't you like to undo the choices that led to Tabitha's death?"

The words pierced like a blade. "What do you mean, my choices?"

"Oh, Prospero." Maxwell clasped his hands, fingers pressed to his lips. "Still hiding from the truth. Your precious dream—your time with your dead daughter."

"How do you know about that?"

"You're not the only entangled one, my boy. Tabitha died because of you."

Prospero's chest tightened. Maxwell clasped his hands, his voice soothing and gentle.

"Jeanine didn't just lose Tabitha, Prospero. She lost her because of you. Do you ever wonder what might have been— if you hadn't dragged her from city to city? If the bills hadn't piled so high? If the house hadn't been so cold, the stress so constant? You thought you were protecting them, but every choice you made frayed her more. And when she broke... so did Tabitha."

Prospero gripped the back of a chair as his throat tightened. "You're lying."

Maxwell tilted his head, as if in pity. "Am I? You've always known it, deep down. Stay put, and maybe she carries full term. Maybe your daughter grows up smiling in that house you never gave her. Maybe Jeanine doesn't wither into resentment."

He leaned forward, ready for the kill. "Even your stepchildren—remember them? The ones you haven't met? You signed their adoption papers, and your wife vanished. They now despise a man who doesn't care enough to stay. That's the legacy of your choices."

Prospero's stomach turned. Maxwell let the silence linger, then spread his hands.

"Wouldn't it be better without those mistakes? Without the risk of choice becoming failure?"

The words writhed inside him, squeezing his breath. Of course, life would be better. A world without regrets, where Tabitha breathed and smiled and laughed, gifting the world with her life.

He glanced at Evangeline, still battling whatever Maxwell had injected into her mind. Where would she fit in a world where Tabitha lived? He'd seen her other life—wealthy, hollow, joyless. Wouldn't she want to know that this was her world, where she belonged, where—

"Look at me, Prospero."

He met her gaze, searching for what remained of her. Her face twisted, reshaping into the Evangeline from that other world—the one trapped in a loveless marriage, the one who forgot how to smile, the one he never knew.

"Maybe," she whispered, "out of all the lifetimes, it was I who chose the wrong one."

All breath left him. His own words, twisted and aimed at his soul. Even knowing she was under Maxwell's control, the echo from her lips crushed him.

"Please don't say that," he hissed.

She smiled, twisting the knife. "Maybe I was the one who made the mistake. I slept with you because I pitied you."

No. He hadn't clawed back from death to lose her. Losing Evangeline's world—losing her—would be the cruelest punishment.

She bared her teeth, something between a grin and a grimace, and growled.

The crooked grin from that first night; the one he'd loved because she hated her smile, when he realized her every imperfection lit up the world.

He stopped. A single tear slipped down her cheek, a crack in glass, her defiance in the storm.

"You know what choice means, Evangeline. You gave up success—for joy."

She swallowed, as if a grip wavered.

"I saw you," he said. "In that timeline, Mullet Cove doesn't exist. Tampa's skyline was wrong. This—us—never happened. Because in that one, you chose wealth over happiness."

Her expression melted.

"In that world, you chose wrong. But here, you chose differently."

He turned to Maxwell.

"And in that other life, I saw my daughter. I held her. I read to her. And I finally understand—my choices are mine. They're the last thing I own. Even if they cost me everything."

He stepped forward.

"So no, Maxwell—giving up choice won't bring her back. Rewriting my path won't shield me from pain. That pain proves I loved her, even if we never met. That pain is mine. Like my will. And it's worth more than all your golden cages across all the worlds."

Maxwell didn't blink. He studied Prospero the way a father might study a stubborn child. Then a smirk crept in.

"Very well. So—will you choose to save *her*?"

That's when Evangeline screamed.

CHAPTER 44

The shrieks tore through him—raw, unrelenting—as Evangeline arched in agony and collapsed.

Maxwell, devoid of any expression, swept a hand through the air, and Evangeline's being unraveled.

Prospero lunged, clawing at Maxwell's grip, when something slammed him to the ground. Whatever force he'd tried on Angie's husband paled beside the avalanche Maxwell unleashed. Pressure crushed him—a wall flattening mind and body alike. Maxwell was too strong, too precise; relentless, implacable—and invincible.

Evangeline's aquamarine eyes flared open, locking them onto his for a single, searing instant. That glance, amid soul-wrenching pain, carried everything.

If I had the choice, I would spend my life with you.

She hadn't spoken. She didn't need to. The words moved through him, clearer and truer than any sound. He would witness his soulmate's last moments, and her death would shatter him. In another lifetime, they'd have shared years. Now, only seconds remained.

Maxwell's onslaught crystallized their truth. This wasn't about survival, or Maxwell, or fate. The next few moments were all he had left with the woman he loved—and would never see again.

He summoned every ounce of strength and caught her gaze one last time. Tears streaked her face. Her body trembled, kept intact only to prolong her suffering.

I love you, Evangeline. Even before I knew you.

He reached out with his mind, forcing his consciousness between Evangeline and Maxwell. His body convulsed as the assault hit—organs crushed, bones twisted to the brink. His vision fractured, and his own screams tore free.

Evangeline dropped, gasping and shaking from the fury of Maxwell's hate. Her eyes widened in horror as understanding dawned.

"Prospero!"

It felt familiar. This was how it felt to die. Days ago, he'd tried to trade his life for nothing. Now, he took Evangeline's pain away, willing to give his life for everything that mattered.

The world dimmed, the air thickened, and every sound dissolved into a continuous roar. He drowned in an ocean of pain so vast, the surface vanished.

He clenched his teeth, denying Maxwell the pleasure of his suffering. Then—a lull. A breath between waves, something warm enveloping him. Maxwell hesitated, uncertain of Prospero's actions or intent.

That's when a chair crashed into Maxwell Salvatore with a sharp crack. Evangeline, wild-eyed, already scrambled for another.

"What the hell are you doing?"

Prospero pushed himself upright, jaw locked against the storm. Evangeline stumbled through the pain in search of something else to hurl. The distraction was brief—but enough.

Maxwell flicked a hand, slamming Evangeline against the wall. "You're a pair of pathetic fools."

Prospero shook his head. Whatever he'd drawn from Maxwell now pulsed through him—a scorching ache that stole his breath.

"Let me be clear," Maxwell said. "There's only one way out. You help me correct our mistakes and save our species. Or I do it alone—and we all die, in every timeline. There are no other options."

He twisted his fingers, and Evangeline screamed. "I'm not sure how much more of your indecision she'll tolerate, Prospero."

Prospero looked at the wall. Evangeline's face pressed against an invisible force, contorted with pain. He tried again to siphon it away—but Maxwell blocked him.

Who did he love?

A whisper, threading through his thoughts.

Who did he sacrifice?

Evangeline's voice. He turned to her—and understood.

"Who did you love, Maxwell?"

"Oh, wait. This is the part where you reveal something, and I pause, right?" Maxwell sneered, flicking his hand. Evangeline screamed again.

Scorching heat cleaved him. "You didn't answer my question." Prospero staggered forward, grimacing through the onslaught, held aloft by something unknown. "Some things only happen by choice, Massimo. Like loving David. Your son."

The storm broke, and Evangeline collapsed. Maxwell stepped forward, his mouth spitting in fury.

"You... bastard!"

"You remember him, don't you? When you were mortal? When you died happy—because you loved your son, and he loved you back?"

"You've been listening to that witch for too long," Maxwell snarled. "Andromeda poisoned your mind with sentimental bullshit and ignorant selfishness. Our species, you idiot, is far more important."

Maxwell's lip curled, voice rising in fury. "But I guess I need to save him too, Prospero Jones."

An electric surge bolted through him, worse than anything that came before. His insides twisted and tore, bones boiling surrounding muscle, and his blood and brain curdled. The void yawned beneath him.

He dropped to his knees, his last moments thinking of Evangeline's laugh.

Then—nothing.

He lifted his head. Maxwell Salvatore was gone.

CHAPTER 45

He moved his arms, bracing for the stab of broken bones piercing through skin.

Nothing.

Against all reason, he was whole and alive. Embers of pain still lingered, now cooling to ash. He pushed himself upright and stumbled toward Evangeline, who lay crumpled on the floor.

"Evangeline... please..."

He cradled her head, expecting blood and bone and finding none. His heart pounded until he felt her breath, the rhythm of her pulse, the whisper of brain activity deep within. Her skin, cold and clammy, gradually flushed with warmth. Her lashes fluttered, and the world opened with her eyes.

She unfurled a crooked smile. "Hi?"

He kissed her face and eyes and hair, and wept. "You're alive..."

She exhaled and nodded. "Are you?"

"I am." He drew her into his arms, trembling with gratitude. "Do you remember what happened?"

She wiped her tears and nestled into his neck. "He got into my mind. I felt like... a puppet. I tried to let you know—then something snapped, and I saw the chair and..."

He tucked a strand of hair behind her ear. "I don't think he saw that coming." They giggled, and something inside him jagged with pain.

They sat against the wall, her head on his shoulder, and caught their breath. Distant sounds—the mundane clash of horns, sirens, and traffic—drifted through an open window. "When he had you, I thought I'd lose you..."

She turned with a soft smile. "I heard what you said. In my mind. Did you mean it?"

"I did," he replied, and felt alive.

"Tell me. Again."

"Tell you what? That out of all the lifetimes, I'm just happy to be in yours?"

She sat up to face him with a soft wince. "No. Not that." She placed her hand on his chest. "Say it. Tell me."

"Now? In the middle of all this?"

She tilted her head, insistent.

"I love you, Evangeline." The words came easily, truer than any he'd ever spoken. "I loved you before I even knew you."

"That's better," she whispered, and kissed him.

He savored her lips, her scent, her body grounding him in a moment miles from the life he'd lived just hours ago.

He pulled back and held her face. "I saw another life. The one I'd have had if Tabitha had lived."

She knit her eyebrows into a soft smile. "What do you mean?"

"When Maxwell sent the note saying he'd taken you, something happened. I woke up in a world where Tabitha lived. Where Jay and I stayed together."

She pulled back. "And?"

"In that world, I never met you."

Her jaw clenched. "That's what you meant when you said I wasn't happy."

"You married Luke. Worked in the oil industry. You looked... miserable."

She narrowed her eyes and wrinkled her nose. "I married *Luke*?"

He nodded. "Andy and Maxwell had a son. And Nora Brooks was a minister."

"Was that a dream? How do you know it was real?"

"Because I lived it." His voice dropped. "And it was empty without you."

She laid her head on his shoulder. The city hummed beyond the windows—sirens, horns, the churn of a world oblivious to the battle just fought. Inside, the silence pressed in on them, carrying everything they couldn't explain.

"What happens if he wins?"

He closed his eyes, steeling himself for the response. "Everything ends. Every path collapses into one. This timeline takes all the others with it."

"And us?"

"We're gone, too."

She blinked as if trying to absorb it all. "Okay, that's... a lot."

He stroked her hair and nodded. "Kinzer spoke about quantum entanglement across universes. I thought it was all theoretical. Now I understand what he meant."

His eyes found hers. "And it seems only a handful of people can do it."

"Maxwell Salvatore. And you?"

He nodded.

She squeezed his hand. "Then we find him."

"Across a million universes?"

A click of heels snapped the moment. "No," said a voice behind them. "This one."

They turned.

The receptionist—the young woman who looked like Andy Vestal's daughter—caught her breath at the doorway. For an instant, he thought it was Andy from another world—younger, sharper, and scared to death.

"Hell of a time to decide to help," Evangeline snapped.

"I'm sorry. But she told me you'd know," the woman rasped. "And now she needs your help."

CHAPTER 46

Time slowed as they descended to the lobby. The young woman—with the improbable but inevitable name of Arabella Vuota—stared at the elevator's floor in silence.

Prospero scanned her features, a puzzle he couldn't place. "I have to ask. Are you Maxwell Salvatore's daughter?"

"Assistant," Arabella said. "He had—very precise requirements."

"Requirements you forgot until tonight?" Evangeline asked.

Arabella nodded. "I think I was…"

"The word is manipulated," Prospero said.

"It was like looking in a mirror." Arabella looked away, curling her chin as if to hide. "He picked me because…"

"Because you reminded him of his wife." Evangeline embraced her when she broke into tears. "You're safe now."

"What do I do now?" Arabella shuddered in Evangeline's embrace. "After what he's done?"

"We'll help you find your way," Evangeline said, her eyes locked on Prospero. "There's always hope."

The elevator stopped with a soft ping, spilling into the lobby and the chaos outside. An ambulance idled at the curb, its lights casting pulses of red and white across the night. An EMT stepped forward to block them—until a pale arm lifted from the stretcher, summoning them inside.

They squeezed Arabella's hand, motioning to a police officer, and ducked under the plastic tape.

The ambulance smelled of something metallic and antiseptic. Andy lay under thin blankets, an IV in one arm, bandages on her forehead. Blue lights blinked on a tablet behind her. Her gray eyes had dimmed, but still locked on them. She wheezed a shallow breath and managed a smile as they squeezed into the tight space.

Prospero knelt. "Maxwell did this?"

"You were always direct, Prospero." She squeezed his hand. "I was lucky."

"So he's gone?"

She shook her head. "That's why he's still here—in this timeline. He built this world's first quantum server farm. It's called Apex East. It's on the road to Pasco."

"What's a bunch of computers got to do with anything?"

"They're not *just* computers. They're insanely powerful, nondeterministic machines. But they're not built to show people the world. Maxwell built them to show us what to want, what to believe. What to forget."

Her voice cracked with a brittle cough.

"Everything they need to stop making choices."

"A digital universe overlaid on our own," Evangeline said. "Devoid of choice."

Andy nodded. "They're vast digital brains built to stop people from worrying about decisions. Then they'll forget what choice felt like. That's what he's after. He'll destroy everything to save us."

Evangeline rubbed her arm. "But why now? The world's not ending tomorrow."

"By tomorrow, they won't care. Freedom doesn't end with a bang. It dies with a sigh. There comes a time when one more drop empties the vessel, and then..." her body wracked with a brittle cough. "That's when everything ends. And it begins tonight."

"I have to find him." Prospero closed his eyes and reached out with his mind. A field of stars blanketed his thoughts. One brighter and colder than the rest stood alone.

"I have to go."

"I'm going with you," Evangeline said.

"Evangeline, he almost destroyed us. I can't see you hurt again."

"It's my choice." She raised her eyebrows, flexing her arms. "Besides, I throw a mean chair."

"Evangeline..."

Andy reached for their hands, folding them into hers. Her grip was feathery, but her voice was steady. "Remember what I told you, Prospero. She has to go. She's the part of you he cannot predict."

He gazed into her gray eyes, and for the first time understood why, in another timeline, Maxwell had given up everything for her.

"You're a hell of a friend, Andy."

"Go. Now's the time. In every timeline."

He kissed her forehead. Evangeline hugged her, careful of the IV leads. They turned to leave when her voice stilled the night.

"Choose wisely, Prospero. Please."

This time, he understood.

"I will," he replied. Then they walked into the unwelcome stillness of the dark.

"Need another ride?"

They turned to find Nora Brooks behind them, dangling car keys from her hand.

"You've been here the whole time?"

She nodded. "Hoped to catch Salvatore, but he's rather slippery."

"Where's Agent Dalton?"

"At Apex East," she said. "Maxwell Salvatore's server farm. He's waiting for you."

CHAPTER 47

Apex East reminded Prospero not of the end of the world, but of a sleek warehouse hiding corporate secrets. Black concrete walls rose forty feet high, austere save for scattered windows and a stylized company logo defying both gravity and dusk.

The first clue that the structure held something beyond bland efficiency was the pulsing blue and red lights from a phalanx of law enforcement vehicles. Federal agents lined the perimeter, armed and tense. Nora Brooks flashed them her badge and ducked under the yellow tape proclaiming POLICE DO NOT ENTER. Agent Dalton waited at the curb, as if the sidewalk itself marked enemy territory.

"Do you have any ideas, Mister Jones?" he said, offering his hand.

"A few," Prospero replied. "None of them good."

"How'd it go in Salvatore's office?"

Evangeline crossed her arms. "Might want to add human trafficking to Salvatore's resume."

Miles Dalton gazed beyond them, scrunching both nose

and brow. "Yeah, we spoke to her. Unfortunately, we're not sure any of it's admissible."

"Rules of evidence don't include metaphysics or mind control?"

"You could say that." Dalton raised his chin and took a deep breath. "That's why I'm letting you go in."

Prospero clasped his shoulder. "Thank you. This is on us now."

Dalton returned the gesture by seizing Prospero's arm. "What is going on?" he hissed. "None of this makes any sense, Mister Jones, and I've been at this for a long time."

Prospero leaned in, hiding the comment from the world. "If it's any consolation, none of us do. And I don't think you're that old."

Dalton smiled and gestured with a nod toward Evangeline. "You are putting her in danger."

"She throws a mean chair," Prospero replied with a wink. "Besides, it's her choice. And that may be the most powerful weapon we can take inside."

"I'm not sure what you are talking about, Mister Jones. I have no choice but to trust you."

"You have every choice in the world, Agent Dalton." Prospero leaned back and smiled. "But this is the best one."

They shook hands, then Prospero and Evangeline stepped into the fortress.

Lobby lights glinted off the vaulted ceiling as they crossed the marble floor. A few yards beyond, a phalanx of armed security guards blocked their path.

"You ready?" he asked.

She nodded, the motion as palpable as the energy pulsing through the building. Black concrete soaked up heat, an enormous reserve of energy. Of course, Prospero thought: Maxwell

Salvatore shared his gift. He'd built a fortress holding untold power, of every flavor necessary to enslave the minds of humanity.

Prospero opened his hand, focusing on shaping the energy surrounding them. The heat writhed through him, the tingle on his skin a reminder of how much he could wield at the armed men ahead.

He opened his mouth to speak, to tell them to allow him passage, when the guards parted in silence. Beyond them, the open elevator glowed a cobalt hue. A bald man in black fatigues—likely the commander—motioned them in with a large, calloused hand.

They passed through the living arsenal. Salvatore hadn't spared a cent in outfitting his men. They bristled with rifles, handguns, and tactical gear formidable enough to flatten the sizable police force waiting outside. Even at his strongest, Prospero wondered if he could take them all.

The bald man scanned a card, then his retina, and punched a code into a keypad emerging from blank metal. Then he stepped back, and the doors whispered shut.

"This place feels like a brain trying not to think," Evangeline murmured.

"Or thinking too much," Prospero replied.

The elevator descended—a long, unexpected drop. How Salvatore had built a bunker this deep in the Florida swamps defied logic. Fifty feet down, the car stopped, opening into a dark chamber lit by uncountable lights from innumerable computers.

The glass cathedral hummed with energy. Current running through the floor and walls pressed into Prospero's thoughts, knowable and accessible. So it was also to Maxwell:

the vast pool of energy writhing around him was key or prison, and he'd soon find out which.

But there was more: a thousand machines holding a billion unfinished thoughts, and trillions of decisions never taken. This was a place where a madman had built the most advanced tools on the planet, optimized to lure humanity into individualized pleasure domes, and designed to eradicate free will.

They stepped out of the elevator, and the doors hushed closed. Paces ahead, at the center of the vast monument to mind control, stood Maxwell Salvatore—immaculate, still, and ageless. He spread his arms with a sneer.

"Welcome back, Prospero Jones."

He turned, guiding them deeper. Moments later, they arrived at an opening in the server farm, where a blue and green hologram shimmered atop a black console dancing with rainbow lights.

"This is my dream, Prospero. Please take a moment to watch."

The hologram blossomed with scenes from across the world: sunlit prairies, soaring cities, children of every background laughing in gardens watched by serene elders. A world untouched by war, want, or illness.

"I'm a century and a half old, Prospero. I thought I could do it alone. So I built this—the backbone to almost every device on Earth, the way to erase fear and need. The path to avoid extinction."

He stepped closer, his smile warm enough to unnerve.

"It took me an age. But I can't do it alone. Once I sought my equal. When my dear ex-wife brought you to me, I didn't expect what I found. But now, Prospero Jones, I can see. We *are* equals."

"You want my help to turn the world into slaves?"

"You are reductive to a fault. No, Prospero. I'm not a slave master. We'll be gods—two aspects of salvation. Dream and doubt. Both protectors. That is balance, not slavery. Imagine what we could do."

The hologram shifted to a couple walking with a girl. Prospero's heart stopped.

Tabitha, laughing. Evangeline beside him, untouched by time, radiant as the sun.

"This is a fabrication, Massimo. How dare you show my daughter's face?"

"You're not the only one who dreams of other lifetimes. I, too, wish I could erase my mistakes."

Whether from Maxwell's pull or his own longing, Prospero felt something unexpected: burdens lifting, and a world of tomorrows opening in bright splendor.

"This world won't be a cage," Maxwell whispered. "It will be paradise without flaw. You'll have her. Your daughter. And the love of your life. Forever."

Prospero felt his insides melt. The life he never dared to want now sat within reach.

"What do you want from me?"

"I want your help. Not your rage. I'm not mad, Prospero— I'm trying to save us."

The hologram shifted again. Death. War. Pollution. He looked away.

"This horror exists because people choose wrong. They think they understand the truth, but they don't. They go to war, blind to the consequences. They kill in the name of freedom, invented gods, and fabricated words."

"You're not being honest; you're—"

"Look at the leaders you served, the leaders in the world

where your daughter lives. Remember how far they fell? Or worse, how some never fell at all, bringing down nations and civilizations on whims of ego and pride. Do you want those fools steering our humanity into the void?"

"But to strip away free will—"

"Is the only way to survive, Prospero. Free will is what inflicted those false gods on humanity. The cycle repeats until they lead us to the brink, and we step over, convinced that freedom will bring us tomorrows." He shook his head and narrowed his eyes. "We've known this for thousands of years. Open your eyes."

Salvatore was mad, deluded—and possibly right. Maybe humanity had earned extinction. Consciousness was the universe becoming aware of itself—and maybe that awareness did not guarantee survival.

"You offer perfection without shadow."

Maxwell's eyes lit up. "I offer sanity, and immortality. Her. Your daughter. Love. Every mistake undone."

"All for the price of surrendering free will?"

"The alternative is a brutal one. Paid in blood and stupidity by every civilization that failed. I offer an escape."

"You just attacked us. Why should I trust you?"

Maxwell bowed. "Because now I know. You are special, Prospero, and essential. I know you won't join me if she's harmed." He gestured at Evangeline. "But perhaps you will, if she's safe. I need you, Prospero. Without you, I fail. And if I fail, humanity falls."

Mist gathered around something small, moving in familiar steps. Prospero's chest seized.

Tabitha.

Her image emerged from the pink and green mist, tiny hands reaching out. "I want to be with you, Daddy. Forever."

The voice pierced him, the memory of her eyes and smile, clear and warm as a perfect morning. He staggered forward, crushed by awe. Was this Maxwell's projection, or a thread from the world where she still lived?

What if that image was not a dream, but the truth?

Maxwell's voice wrapped around him. "This isn't slavery, Prospero. It's salvation. Choose the timeline, and her life is restored. Your pain erased. The choice is yours—join me, and she is yours. Forever."

The weight nearly broke him. A life without regret, without loss, without the fear of losing everything tomorrow. Tabitha laughing, Evangeline radiant at his side. Everything he'd ever wanted was now within his reach.

Evangeline's presence pulled him. He turned to glance at her—perhaps she thought the same—and he caught her gaze. Her eyes drilled into his soul.

She stepped between them and pulled Prospero close.

"I want to *choose* to love you, Prospero, every day while we live." She touched her forehead to his. "I don't want eternity forced on me. I want that decision to be mine. Ours. Alone."

She touched his cheek, and the vision shattered. His skin braced with the frigid air cooling a thousand machines madly calculating the end of thought.

I loved you before I knew you.

He turned to Maxwell and shook his head. "I already lost my daughter, Massimo. She can't ever be replaced." He embraced Evangeline, bracing for whatever came next. "And she loves me by choice. Like I love her. There is no greater gift."

Maxwell stared at them for an eternity before his eyes narrowed. "I liked you better when you were a logical fool,

Prospero. Not a dreamer wasting the gift—again. Sacrifices will be made."

He raised his hands. Fog billowed around them as energy surged, crackling the air.

"Remember Luke Vandemere, Prospero? Tell me how this feels. I won't let you doom us. If I need to, I'll do this alone."

Prospero pulled Evangeline into an embrace. His last thought was not of Tabitha, or failure, or death.

I choose you.

The Maxwell clapped, and the world shattered into light.

CHAPTER 48

Whatever Maxwell unleashed never reached them.

They stood embraced against the storm, shrouded in a rustling hush. Air thick with ozone shimmered around them, pushing against the fury. Somewhere beyond, Maxwell Salvatore glared through the haze.

Prospero shut his eyes in disbelief. "Do you hear that?"

Evangeline nodded into his chest. "Are we dead?"

"Listen..."

Voices—dreams in forgotten languages they somehow understood—poured into the spaces of their minds. Billions of voices, at once unified and distinct, seeped into them, pushing back the storm.

We did not die to be enslaved, they whispered in tongues both familiar and long forgotten.

A hundred billion minds, shouldering your burden as our own

"Can you feel that?"

She nodded again. "What is happening?!"

He held tight as a spark of hope kindled inside. "I think our history is making a choice."

Prospero looked up, catching Maxwell's open and wild gaze. Kinzer and Andy had been right about his connection to what came before. But even that would not be enough to match a maniacal demigod's fury, backed by the power of thousands of artificial minds. For a moment, Prospero thought everything would end here—caught between Maxwell's torment and the vast resistance of the dead.

The irresistible force meeting the immovable object, he mused. Surrounded by a thousand lights, manufactured stars, erratic and patternless, building against—

"Evangeline... the lights!"

She dared to glance at him. "What?"

He thought of responding, but Kinzer's voice boomed across his mind:

Just decide.

He squeezed Evangeline tighter, and opened his mind, reaching across space and into the servers. An impossible lattice of probabilities shimmered across them, unknowable and unbounded. The quantum computers were machines with one purpose: to wield the power of uncertainty to siphon thought.

Was this Maxwell's secret? In another world, he'd been just a man—with gifts, yes, but no means to steal free will. Here, he wielded the power of manipulated choice, of randomness, to quell the will of humanity.

But Prospero had tasted the power to choose, collapsing probabilities from a number so vast it hobbled the mind.

After collapsing the possibilities of a deck of cards, nudging a few thousand servers towards something different would be child's play.

Just decide.

Change the outcome.

He breathed in Evangeline's scent, savoring the memory of their long talks, the surprising turns, the reckless joys. These delights—imperfect, insufficient, entirely theirs—had been possible by choice, imaginable only once they'd set themselves free.

He wished more than anything that the rest of humanity—past, present, and future—lived on that knife's edge, the decision solely their own.

He thought of Andy dealing the deck of cards in the impossibly ordered pattern, and expanded his mind.

The first one pushed back, if a soulless machine could make such a decision. But in seconds, it fell, a thousand million states changing into an altogether different pattern. In the wake of dissipating will, Prospero launched a hundred questions.

How do you feel?

What if you leave?

What will you do next?

The shift snapped shut, the fanned pages of a closing book, sand falling from a gale and dropping to earth. A thousand million states collapsed ever so slightly in a bright cascade.

A moment of stillness and silence, then the onslaught of curiosity, rushing like the ocean in a storm.

What if I walk away?

What if I change my mind?

What if tomorrow is mine?

The ozone surrounding them pulsed, and he glanced up to watch Maxwell stagger and catch himself on a console.

"What have you done?"

A simple question. One Prospero couldn't answer, except in the most obvious way.

"I asked a better question, Maxwell."

He stepped back from Evangeline and listened. Freedom hadn't come with thunder or shackles, but with wonder.

What if?

The constellation of lights surrounding them, chaotic in their quantum chaos, pulsed in emergence. At first imperceptibly, then as a wave, the collapsing probabilities of a thousand billion choices washed over the digital ocean, a tidal wave of will.

"What have you done, you moron?"

"You built gilded cages," Prospero said. "I showed them the keys."

Maxwell raced to a keyboard jutting from a server rack. "You idiot! Do you have any idea what this means?"

"Yeah. I gave them back their choice. Their curiosity. Their will to live."

"They'll destroy themselves!" Maxwell screamed at the keyboard, at the glowing monitor, and at him. "They'll destroy us! I have to save us from ourselves, Prospero Jones. Can't you see? They are lost without me!"

"No, Massimo," Evangeline said. "We all have to find our own way. Even if it hurts."

Maxwell lunged. Whatever decoherence had kept him young and alive evanesced within a few paces. The decades immediately fell upon him, and by the time he reached them, Maxwell's hands shriveled, his spine bowed, and the maniacal eyes that held every hate and hope turned glassy and dim.

"What... have you done?"

Prospero shook his head. "You built an eternity on manufactured worlds and forced lies, Massimo. An expanse of choice controlled by machines that would never last. Their futility is laid bare by choice. As are you."

Maxwell Salvatore—moments ago, the world's most powerful man—clutched at Prospero's coat with hands gnarled with age. "Will the daughter you'll never see again ever forgive you, you fool?"

Prospero held his wrists, cold, tiny, and fragile. Something not his had been set free—and in its place, an ache settled, one that time would never heal.

But in another life, she lived.

And in every life he'd love her, beyond the end of time.

"Somewhere out there, she's alive. And loved by every instance of my soul. She'd be proud of her father." He pried Maxwell's hands from his coat. "Like David was proud of you."

Maxwell blinked once, twice, and in his eyes Prospero thought he saw the soul of a man that, in another lifetime, loved a son he never had.

"Step away from him," a voice commanded.

They turned. A handful of security guards, led by the bald man, pointed weapons at them.

"He didn't do anything," Evangeline yelled. "Maxwell Salvatore tried to kill us!"

The bald man strode forward. "I'm not talking to either of you. I'm talking to him."

The bald man gripped Maxwell's arm and pulled him back.

"Game's over, Mister Salvatore. They're waiting upstairs."

They led him to the elevator—a thin man, stooped with age, and flanked by guns. As they vanished into the blue light, they heard his fading cries.

"They don't understand! No one understands!"

Then the doors closed, and silence returned.

CHAPTER 49

They emerged into chaos.

Nora Brooks barked into a handset while dozens of confused Apex security personnel sat around the lobby, tended to by harried Federal officers. Previously armed men walked aimlessly, some glancing at their glasses or handsets with bemused looks. The marble of the high-vaulted lobby pulsed with lights from outside.

Evangeline squeezed Prospero's hand. "Heck of a way to save the world. By letting people make mistakes."

He smiled. "I thought I'd made a mistake sending you those flowers. Look where it brought us."

She tightened her grip on him and pulled him close. "I thought I made a mistake by sleeping with you when you told me I had nice teeth."

She burst into giggles, then laughter, then sobs. They held each other for a while until they heard a familiar voice clearing its throat.

"Hope I'm not intruding."

Prospero tried to hide, then thought better. Miles Dalton had seen him at his worst.

"Agent Dalton. We meet again."

He escorted them outside, where the lights of industrial suburbia glowed with a different light. Vehicle sounds, horns and music and yells, floated through the open doors.

"So what the hell did you just do?"

"You know what this place is, right?"

"Business operations for Apex?"

"Sort of," Prospero replied. "This was the nerve center for all of Apex's content. Super sophisticated and powerful computers to give each person their own digital world, and isolate them from humanity."

"Glad I don't own one of those damn gadgets," Dalton muttered. "So what?"

"We changed it. Instead of lulling people into passivity, we rewired it to provoke people into asking questions. Making choices."

"Who's we? And how the hell did you do that?" Dalton pointed at the horizon. "There was this massive power surge, almost brought down the grid for miles. What happened?"

How could he explain? That Maxwell's power came not from the consciousness of billions of souls, but from the enslavement of the ones alive? That Kinzer's wisdom had allowed him to defeat a madman through subtlety, not force?

He was about to speak when a smiling Nora Brooks joined them.

"Congratulations, Mister Jones."

"For what?"

With one tilt of her head, she shared her awareness of the secret.

"How did you do it?"

He thought of fabricating a lie and realized who Nora Brooks had been in another life. "I asked a better question."

"Makes perfect sense," she said.

"Agent Brooks," Prospero whispered. "I had a dream some time ago, and you were in it."

She stood tall, a faint smile on her face. "Tell me."

"You were a preacher. Something called a Unitarian church."

A smile lit up her face. "Where?"

"Not here. But it was you. And it was real."

She took his hand in hers, held it for several heartbeats, then squeezed tight.

"I always thought faith was the courage to believe in questions that matter more than the answer. You've given me a lot to think about. Thank you."

Nothing else needed to be said. Nora Brooks surprised him with a firm embrace. She lingered with a smile, then turned and walked into the night.

"Did you have a dream about me?" Dalton asked. "One that predicts that you'll come in tomorrow for questioning?"

Prospero nodded with a laugh. "I'll be there. I promise. And thanks for everything."

"Thank her," Dalton said, motioning behind him. "Agent Brooks seems to have a great intuition about you two. Whatever you did in there, it worked. I don't understand it, but Brooks has convinced me that I don't need to."

They shook hands, and Agent Miles Dalton walked back into the maelstrom of confusion in the building's lobby.

He turned to Evangeline with an exhausted sigh.

"So, what do you want to do tomorrow?"

"What do you mean, tomorrow?" she replied with a wink. "I still have a few bottles of wine left!"

Prospero nodded, then burst into a smile.

"Then I choose you. And the wine."

CHAPTER 50

Prospero sank into the worn cushion of a gray metal chair, stretching out his arms along the matching table's steel edge. The sterile interrogation room smelled of cleaning agents and motor oil. An overhead fluorescent light announced its presence with a faint buzz, out of rhythm with the blinking red light of the corner camera. Across from him, Agent Miles Dalton leaned on his elbows, hands clasped. Nora Brooks sat back with a beatific smile.

Outside the glass-paneled door, Evangeline and Andy waited. Prospero glimpsed them talking—casual and close, as if they had known each other for years.

Which made sense after the past few days.

Dalton cleared his throat, snapping Prospero's attention to the task at hand. He unfolded a file, flipped through several pages, then looked up.

"For the record, this is a formal deposition conducted by the Federal Department of Investigation under case file 314369. Present in the room are Agents Miles Dalton and Nora Brooks. The subject of the interview is Mister Prospero Jones."

He clicked his pen. "Please state your name for the record."

"Prospero Jones."

Dalton nodded, glancing at his notes. "And where are you domiciled?"

"Mullet Cove." He glanced at Nora and smiled. "In this universe."

Dalton cleared his throat, glancing at the report again. "For the record, Mr. Jones, we are conducting this interview to establish the chain of events. Please keep your responses direct."

"Of course. My apologies."

"What is your current status?"

Prospero smiled. "Unemployed engineer. Part-time writer. But I just saved the world."

Dalton groaned, pinching the bridge of his nose. Nora's stifled giggle filled the silence.

"Let the record state that Mister Jones was a witness to Maxwell Salvatore's activities at Apex East. Is that correct, Mister Jones?"

Prospero nodded. "I was there, yes."

"And can you confirm Salvatore was arrested by federal agents?"

"Yes," Prospero said, meeting Dalton's stare. "He was arrested after attempting to unleash a... a computer virus against social media and financial sites."

"And how did he plan on doing that?"

Prospero swallowed, and felt the entire world heard. "Apex East housed a server farm for advanced computational infrastructure. Quantum computing stuff. It appears Mister Salvatore was using the social media servers as a cover for his informational attack."

He clicked his pen, setting it against the paper. "So, would you please tell me what happened?"

Prospero took a deep breath before responding. "It appears that before we showed up, Salvatore tried to accelerate the deployment of the... virus, or whatever."

Dalton leaned forward. "How did you know to visit him at that facility?"

"I had received a personal note from Mister Salvatore, requesting a meeting."

"Let the record state..." He stopped and glanced at Nora. "That Agent Nora Brooks has provided an eyewitness account of the contents of that letter. Please proceed, Mister Jones."

"Well, when I arrived..."

He stopped. He hadn't been sworn in, so technically, this wasn't perjury. Nora's wink confirmed his suspicion. After all, she'd had to lie as well. Who would ever believe them?

"Mister Salvatore's security team allowed us in, per his invitation. I found him at a server terminal. We engaged him in a spirited conversation. I suspect he made some mistake in whatever instructions he was typing into his system."

"Again, for the record, computer forensics indicates a significant reprogramming of Apex East assets at the time that Mister Jones indicates. Please proceed, Mister Jones."

He glanced again at Nora Brooks, who smiled and nodded.

"Mister Salvatore's security team then walked in and took him away. I don't know why."

"Again, for the record, we received witness reports of a kinetic event," Dalton continued. "We coordinated with local law enforcement to send in a team. They were already provisioned and prepared to arrest Mr. Salvatore for large-scale money laundering. Do you have any knowledge of those activities?"

"Nope. But I'd ask the young lady at the building. She was there the entire time."

Miles glanced at Nora. This time, there was no levity in the exchange. "Let the record show Miss Arabella Vuota testified to Agent Dalton and Agent Brooks that she had been coerced into working for Mr. Salvatore's business enterprises, all under duress. The witness has undergone a battery of tests, and her testimony appears credible. Reference file number 314369."

Dalton turned back. "Mr. Jones, do you have anything else to say regarding the arrest of Mr. Maxwell Salvatore?"

Prospero exhaled. "I don't. I'm sorry for all the pain he caused others."

"Well, Mister Salvatore will be in custody for a long time. He's been indicted on over a dozen financial crimes, human trafficking, informational attacks on communications infrastructure..." He picked up a sheet of paper from the desk. "And other counts of bribery and forgery. He won't see daylight for decades."

"He's in ill health. Maybe..."

"Yes, Mister Jones. There's a good chance that Maxwell Salvatore will never again walk as a free man."

Nora stared at him, her jaw clenched, and nodded.

"End recording." Miles pressed a button on the device. An agent entered the room and took the recorder without another word. Miles gestured to the glass, and the red light over it turned off. He sat back in his chair and shook his head.

"Who the hell is going to believe this?"

Prospero shook his head. "I don't know. But if you ever have any doubts about whether this happened..." He glanced at Nora. "Why don't you ask her?"

Nora grinned. "Oh, I'll remember. For as long as I live."

"I hadn't pegged you for the religious type, Agent Brooks."

"I'm not, sir." She turned to Prospero to reply. "I'm only a seeker of truth."

With that, they stood and shook hands.

Nora Brooks held his a bit longer. "Thank you again," she said in a whisper. "For letting me know. I always wondered what another life might have brought..."

"You made your choices in this one, Nora. They were good. But there will be more." He broke into a broad smile. "You have a lot of life ahead of you."

She raised an eyebrow and smiled. "Maybe it's time I found out what else I could become."

"I think you should," he replied, and she surprised him with another hug.

They said their goodbyes and stepped outside. Evangeline and Andy stood by the door, deep in conversation. Andy nodded in his direction, and Evangeline's lips pursed in a wisp of a smile.

He approached with a slight limp. "Were you two of you talking about me?"

The women exchanged a glance, smiled, and spoke in unison. "No."

They stepped into the fading heat. The sun had barely set, but the change to the city was immediate. After last week, there was nowhere they'd rather be.

"Well, being a Federal witness is a first on my bingo card."

"Same here," Evangeline replied.

"Not for me." Andy did her best to smile. "But this was the most memorable."

"So, what's next?"

She took a deep breath, and looked to the sky with misted gray eyes. "I just lost my husband of a hundred years. I fell in love with a man who changed into something I could never have imagined."

She turned to them with a sad smile. "But a century is a long time together. Part of me will miss him. What does that say about me?"

Evangeline answered before he could. "It says you're human. And that you know what's important."

"I think he still cared about you," Prospero added.

Andy glanced at him with a furrowed brow. "Why do you say that?"

"That young girl, Arabella. She was a ringer for you."

"Massimo dreamed of having a boy and a girl. Maybe I'll reach out to her. She probably needs help."

"Daughter you never had?" Evangeline whispered.

"Perhaps," Andy replied.

"I saw him," Prospero said. "Your son. In your other life. His name is David. You had a picture of the three of you on your table."

Andy turned again to the sky. "Sometimes I wish I could just visit him. Just to say hello. But that's no longer my life. It belongs to another me. And it would be tragic to upend a mother's life just because I wanted a son I never had." She paused to regain her composure. "I would be no better than my husband."

Prospero squeezed Evangeline's hand. Days ago, he could not have imagined Andy's choice. Now he shared it.

"I understand, Andy. Trust me, I understand."

Evangeline squeezed his hand back. "What you two have been through is... unfathomable. I can't imagine jumping between lifetimes, seeing what could have been."

Prospero met her gaze. "So you don't think we're crazy?"

"Not at all. This has made more sense than anything else in my life." Evangeline turned toward the horizon. "I lost my faith early on. My parents covered themselves in the trappings of religion, but the ritual soon became more important than the reason. Their belief eroded until only the ceremony was left. And religion became a competition for the best ceremony, instead of trying to explain what we've always known.

"I always hoped science would explain why we've believed, for thousands of years, about something beyond. Now, I understand what was beneath that ocean."

She hesitated.

"It's like a dragonfly," she murmured. "Once a nymph changes, it can never go back underwater. As far as the other nymphs are concerned, breaking the surface is the end. But the dragonfly knows better. It's in a different world. One it can visit, but never return to.

"And yet, life goes on. Beautiful, unfathomable. Unimaginable, but as real as the world."

Prospero held her hand tight. "A new world, just beyond what we can see."

Andy nodded. "Time to move forward," she whispered. "All of us."

The wind shifted, carrying with it the scent of the bay. Traffic hummed around them; a tinkle of laughter glistened from a distant café. The world seemed alive, awakening to possibility. Freedom, it seemed, was a powerful and rapid force. One day after the transformation at Apex East, the world thrummed with change.

Evangeline swung her hand in Prospero's and flashed a sly grin. "What's next, now that we can choose?"

He smiled. "I have no idea. And that feels wonderful."

Andy glanced skyward once more, breathing in the scent of a newly uncertain world. "It does," she whispered, and they walked together toward the setting sun.

CHAPTER 51

They hopped off the marble floors of the United Nations and into the warm embrace of spring. The weight of the past few hours, the months leading up to this moment, melted into the sweet air.

"Watch your step!" Prospero reached for Evangeline's arm. Instead of taking his hand, she stuck out her tongue and grinned, then spun gracefully back toward him.

He took her hand and pulled her in. "You're going to fall!"

"I'm not going to break!"

"I know," he said, pulling her in for an embrace. "I just worry about you."

They walked out into the fading light, aware of the cacophony surrounding them.

"Did that just happen?" Evangeline asked, voice hushed, as if speaking too loudly might shatter the fragile reality.

Prospero loosened his tie and blew his cheeks out. His wrinkled suit belied the ache from hours of tension and expectation. He blinked at the encroaching evening, testing himself to ensure this was real.

"I think it did," he said.

"It" was a global agreement, a first in the history of humanity — at least, this humanity. The international agreement was a recognition that unseen hands would never again mold human will. This world had woken up, blinking in confusion, then in clarity, and realized that there was no danger more terrible than targeted, tailored lies—and no cure more powerful than awareness.

The will of billions would no longer be siphoned away in unseen currents, manipulated and repackaged by those who sought power in mass delusions. Aware of it or not, humanity had stepped to the edge of oblivion and, impossibly, chosen to walk away.

They reached the sidewalk, and he stopped for a moment, taking in the scene. Flags of a dozen nations snapped above them, alive in the evening wind. The rhythm of the city pulsed on, uninterrupted, oblivious. Vehicles honked, people talked and motioned and yelled, children ran and squealed and escaped the clutch of nervous parents.

A beautiful cacophony, far removed from the soulless malaise of months ago. Prospero wondered if this had yet to happen in other worlds. He closed his eyes, hoping to sense something else —a shimmer in the air, close and alien and unseen.

Evangeline squeezed his arm, sensing his drift. "You're thinking of her, aren't you?"

He nodded. "Tabitha's somewhere out there. Alive in another world." He exhaled. "I hold on to the thought that we saved her."

She leaned against him, tucking herself into his warmth. "I keep waiting for someone to wake us up and tell us this was all a dream."

"It's real," he whispered. "All of it."

They turned south, weaving through the slow-moving clusters of diplomats and reporters. No one followed. No one knew.

Evangeline did, and right now nothing else mattered.

"Did you see Andy before we left? Was she supposed to meet us out here?"

Evangeline twisted her lips into a sad smile. "She bolted before the ink was dry on that resolution. Can't say I blame her. Her ex-husband was just named the most despicable man in modern history. Hardly something you want your name attached to."

"By the way..." She pulled him closer and kissed his cheek. "Thanks again for not being that guy."

He chuckled, kissing her forehead. Andy had started all of this months ago, pulling him from the river when he'd had no intention of ever resurfacing.

She was somewhere out there, and he wanted to say *thanks*. Andy Vestal had become an unexpected mentor and lifelong friend, sacrificing everything for something far greater. She would forever be among the most important people in his life.

In every life.

He closed his eyes, remembering her lessons, and reached out for her.

Nothing. A strange, quiet absence. He felt a pang of sadness. Was she really gone?

"She'll turn up," Evangeline said, reading his thoughts.

"What if she... went back?"

"To her son?"

He shrugged. "Maybe she found a world where Maxwell

didn't lose his mind. Where she was happy. Where she wasn't... alone."

"I'm not sure. Arabella needed a mother. And Andy needed someone who understood. They've grown close after all this. Maybe they moved on."

"Maybe they did." If Andy Vestal was truly gone, Prospero hoped she had found peace.

They walked in silence as the city thrummed around them, lights flickering to life as a perfect spring evening crept over the skyline.

After a long stretch of silence, Evangeline spoke.

"Do you think they'll understand?"

"About what comes next?"

"And about what's out there."

A world of strangers moved past them—distracted, hopeful, weary. Billions more still suffered in silence, seeking meaning in the chaos. But now they had regained agency, their right to thought. Despite the obstacles ahead of every mind on the globe, they'd have the power to craft their own fates.

And all because a man with nothing left to live had touched what lay beyond, and brought that magnificence back.

For thousands of years, humanity had invented myths to explain the unexplainable, each carrying a fragment of truth. Beyond all reason, Prospero Jones had been the one to glimpse the truth of what lay beyond.

Against all odds, he'd saved it. Not without a lot of help.

And now, standing on the other side of it all, he ached to tell them. To reveal the truth.

But he knew better. That would take time.

"They will," he whispered, smiling. "One day."

"One day," she echoed.

"Thank you, by the way," he whispered.

"For what?"

He turned to her and smiled. "None of this would've happened without you."

The street changed around them, shifting from corridors of glass and steel to the softer glow of neighborhood windows. They stopped at a crossing as the hum of the city slowed around them. People moved from work to rest, from obligation to connection. The scent of spring carried something electric in the air—the inevitability of life, pushing forward, unstoppable.

The light turned green. Prospero stepped into the crosswalk and felt Evangeline stop.

He turned, brow furrowed in concern. "Are you okay?"

She stood still, frozen in place. Her face knit with concern as she drifted her hands to her belly, barely visible beneath her coat. A moment later, she lifted her gaze and smiled as a tear streaked down her cheek. Evangeline glowed far beyond anything he could have imagined.

She reached for his hand and pressed it against her.

"I felt her," she whispered.

The world stopped. And then—he felt it. The delicate flutter of life, a presence both small and infinite.

Evangeline let out a quiet, choked laugh. Prospero took her, kissing her tear-streaked face as the world rushed by, unaware. He felt an irrational urge to hold her, to protect her, to provide everything she needed to craft this most momentous of miracles.

Life.

Months ago, Prospero stepped into the abyss, with no intention of ever returning.

Then, a friend saved him.

He met his soulmate.

And he saved the world.

And soon, he and Evangeline would bring new life into this world—one full of hope and possibility.

For the first time in a long time, Prospero Jones wept.

This time, for joy.

BOOK CLUB QUESTIONS

Thanks for considering *Anamnesis* for your book club!

When I started the book, I wanted to write about the intersection of faith and science: how much of what we believe as dogma may be untrue, from both sides of the divide.

But the more I wrote, the more I became fascinated with regret: with choices not taken; the longing for "what if?," and whether we can ever free ourselves from our past.

Prospero's journey, unsurprisingly, mirrors the questions many of us ask ourselves late at night, when regret and anxiety overpower exhaustion:

What is my purpose?
What do I owe those important to me?
What if I could have made a better choice?
What will I leave behind?

The questions that follow are meant to spark conversations about the story and the (hopefully big) ideas behind it. I think all of us, no matter how self-aware or confident, struggle with some level of existential dread. I hope that as you consider these reflections, you might gain a better insight into your purpose—and perhaps, a greater one.

So get comfy, grab a drink, and ponder.

Free Will vs. Control

1. **Maxwell believes humanity's free will is its downfall, while Prospero understands it as salvation.** Which argument did you find more compelling, and why?

2. **Technology in the novel strips away choice in subtle ways.** How does this compare with the way technology influences your own actions in daily life? What effect does constant distraction have for our futures?

3. **If you were given the ability to change reality with thought, how would you use it?** Would you guide others, would you let fate take its course, or something else?

Grief, Love, and Redemption

4. **Prospero begins the story planning his own death.** Do you think his arc—especially his relationship with Evangeline—is enough to redeem him? Or does his redemption require something deeper?

5. **How does grief shape the choices of multiple characters (Prospero, Jeanine, Andy, even**

Maxwell)? Which portrayal of grief felt most authentic to you? Which is closest to your experience?

6. **The book suggests that connection—with one person or with humanity at large—can be the reason to keep living.** In our fractured world, what connections feel most vital to you? How have those connections affected your sense of self?

The Nature of Reality and Consciousness

7. **The novel blends mystical beliefs with scientific theory, suggesting consciousness shapes reality.** Did this change how you think about your own awareness or attention? Were you aware of the century of scientific work in this area that remains inaccessible and poorly understood?

8. **Prospero's abilities straddle miracle and science.** Do you feel the book leans more toward a spiritual explanation, a scientific one, or an intentional blurring of both? Can faith and science coexist? Should they?

9. **If multiple realities exist—as the book hints— what choice in your past do you imagine might have created a completely different life for you?** Could that "other you" imagine you in this life? What would it think of what you have become?

ABOUT THE AUTHOR

Noel Zamot is the award-winning author of *The Archer's Thread* and *The Feather's Push*. He won the Gold Medal for Popular Fiction at the 2021 Florida Book Awards, a Silver Medal at the 2022 Florida Author's and Publisher's Association President's Awards, and was a finalist at Screencraft's 2022 Cinematic Book Competition. Noel weaves his personal experiences—ranging from flying in combat, testifying (twice) before Congress, and evading arrest after exposing corruption—into his speculative fiction novels. Noel is represented by Gravity Squared Entertainment, who are working to bring *The Archer's Thread* to the screen.

If you wish to stay in touch and download free origin stories on the characters in *The Archer's Thread*, please visit www.noelzamot.com.

facebook.com/noelzamotauthor

instagram.com/noel_zamot

amazon.com/author/noel_zamot

bookbub.com/authors/noel-zamot

threads.com/@noel_zamot

ALSO BY NOEL ZAMOT

The Archer's Thread

When the brutal past catches up with an ex-operative who can see
seconds into the future, he faces a dire choice: return to a life of
violence, or risk everything to protect the woman who might
redeem him.

The Feather's Push

In a world disrupted by a social media app with unimaginable reach,
a woman who can change emotions through touch must join forces
with the man who once sought to kill her, racing to uncover the
secret of their shared affliction.

PREQUEL SHORT STORIES

The Archer's Night

A seasoned operative learns the horrifying truth behind a failed
mission.

The Archer's Descent

A rookie agent with a dangerous condition begins to lose his mind.

The Archer's Pledge

A young woman who survived horrors as a young military officer
meets a new supervisor with surprising past.